AUTHOR'S FOREWORD

The theology in this novel is not an analogue of any known religion. It stems from an attempt made by William Sarill and myself to develop an abstract, logical system of religious thought, based on the arbitrary postulate that God exists. I should say, too, that the late Bishop James A. Pike, in discussions with me, brought forth a wealth of theological material for my inspection, none of which I was previously acquainted with.

In the novel, Maggie Walsh's experiences after death are based on an LSD experience of my own. In exact detail.

The approach in this novel is highly subjective; by that I mean that at any given time, reality is seen – not directly – but indirectly, i.e., through the mind of one of the characters. This viewpoint mind differs from section to section, although most of the events are seen through Seth Morley's psyche.

All material concerning Wotan and the death of the gods is based on Richard Wagner's version of *Der Ring des Nibelungen*, rather than on the original body of myths.

Answers to questions put to the tench were derived from the *I Ching,* the Chinese *Book of Changes.*

'Tekel upharsin' is Aramaic for, 'He has weighed and now they divide.' Aramaic was the tongue that Christ spoke. There should be more like him.

CONTENTS

ONE

His job, as always, bored him. So he had during the previous week gone to the ship's transmitter and attached conduits to the permanent electrodes extending from his pineal gland. The conduits had carried his prayer to the transmitter, and from there the prayer had gone into the nearest relay network; his prayer, during these days, had bounced throughout the galaxy, winding up – he hoped – at one of the god-worlds.

His prayer had been simple. 'This damn inventory-control job bores me,' he had prayed. 'Routine work – this ship is too large and in addition it's overstaffed. I'm a useless standby module. Could you help me find something more creative and stimulating?' He had addressed the prayer, as a matter of course, to the Intercessor. Had it failed he would have presently re-addressed the prayer, this time to the Mentufacturer.

But the prayer had not failed.

'Mr Tallchief,' his supervisor said, entering Ben's work cubicle. 'You're being transferred. How about that?'

'I'll transmit a thank you prayer,' Ben said, and felt good inside. It always felt good when one's prayers were listened to and answered. 'When do I transfer? Soon?' He had never concealed his dissatisfaction from his supervisor; there was now even less reason to do so.

'Ben Tallchief,' his supervisor said. 'The praying mantis.'

'Don't you pray?' Ben asked, amazed.

'Only when there's no other alternative. I'm in favour of a person solving his problems on his own, without outside help. Anyhow, your transfer is valid.' His supervisor dropped a document on the desk before Ben. 'A small colony on a planet named Delmak-O. I don't know anything about it, but I suppose you'll find it all out when you get there.' He eyed Ben thoughtfully. 'You're entitled to use one of the ship's nosers. For a payment of three silver dollars.'

'Done,' Ben said, and stood up, clutching the document.

He ascended by express elevator to the ship's transmitter, which he found hard at work transacting official ship business. 'Will you be having any empty periods later today?' he asked the chief radio operator. 'I have another prayer, but I don't want to tie up your equipment if you'll be needing it.'

'Busy all day,' the chief radio operator said. 'Look, Mac – we put one prayer through for you last week; isn't that enough?'

Anyhow I tried, Ben Tallchief mused as he left the transmitter with its hardworking crew and returned to his own quarters. If the matter ever comes up, he thought, I can say I did my best. But, as usual, the channels were tied up by nonpersonal communications.

He felt his anticipation grow; a creative job at last, and just when he needed it most. Another few weeks here, he said to himself, and I would have been pizzling away at the bottle again as in lamented former times. And of course that's why they granted it, he realized. They knew I was nearing a break. I'd probably have wound up in the ship's brig, along with – how many were there in the brig now? – well, however many there were in there. Ten, maybe. Not much for a ship this size. And with such stringent rules.

From the top drawer of his dresser he got out an unopened fifth of Peter Dawson scotch, broke the seal, unscrewed the lid. Little libation, he told himself as he poured scotch into a Dixie cup. And celebration. The gods appreciate ceremony. He drank the scotch, then refilled the small paper cup.

To further enlarge the ceremony he got down – a bit reluctantly – his copy of The Book: A. J. Specktowsky's *How I Rose From the Dead in My Spare Time and So Can You*, a cheap copy with soft covers, but the only copy he had ever owned; hence he had a sentimental attitude toward it. Opening at random (a highly approved method) he read over a few familiar paragraphs of the great twenty-first century Communist theologian's *apologia pro sua vita*.

'God is not supernatural. His existence was the first and most natural mode of being to form itself.'

True, Ben Tallchief said to himself. As later theological investigation had proved. Specktowsky had been a prophet as well as a logician; all that he had predicted had turned up sooner or later. There remained, of course, a good deal to know . . . for example, the cause of the Mentufacturer's coming into being (unless one was satisfied to believe with Specktowsky, that beings of that order were self-creating, and existing outside of time, hence outside of causality). But in the main it was all there on the many-times-printed pages.

'With each greater circle the power, good and knowledge on the part of God weakened, so that at the periphery of the greatest circle his good was weak, his knowledge was weak – too weak for him to observe the Form Destroyer, which was called into being by God's acts of form creation. The origin of the Form Destroyer is unclear; it is, for instance, not possible to declare whether (one) he was a separate entity from God from the start, uncreated by God but also self-creating, as is God, or (two) whether the Form Destroyer is an aspect of God, there being nothing—'

He ceased reading, sat sipping scotch and rubbing his forehead semi-wearily. He was forty-two years old and had read The Book many times. His life, although long, had not added up to much, at least until now. He had held a variety of jobs, doing a modicum of service to his employers, but never ever really excelling. Maybe I can begin to excel, he said to himself. On this new assignment. Maybe this my big chance.

Forty-two. His age had astounded him for years, and each time he had sat so astounded, trying to figure out what had become of the young, slim man in his twenties, a whole additional year slipped by and had to be recorded, a continually growing sum which he could not reconcile with his self-image. He still saw himself, in his mind's eye, as youthful, and when he caught sight of himself in photographs he usually collapsed. For example, he shaved now with an electric razor, unwilling to gaze at himself in his bathroom mirror. Somebody took my actual physical presence away and substituted *this*, he had thought from time to time. Oh well, so it went. He sighed.

Of all his many meagre jobs he had enjoyed one alone, and he still meditated about it now and then. In 2105 he had operated the background music system aboard a huge colonizing ship on its way to one of the Deneb worlds. In the tape vault he had found all of the Beethoven symphonies mixed haphazardly in with string versions of *Carmen* and of Delibes and he had played the Fifth, his favourite, a thousand times throughout the speaker complex that crept everywhere within the ship, reaching each cubicle and work area. Oddly enough no one had complained and he had kept on, finally shifting his loyalty to the Seventh and at last, in a fit of excitement during the final months of the ship's voyage, to the Ninth – from which his loyalty never waned.

Maybe what I really need is sleep, he said to himself. A sort of twilight of living, with only the background sound of Beethoven audible. All the rest a blur.

No, he decided; I want to *be*! I want to act and accomplish something. And every year it becomes more necessary. Every year, too, it slips further and further away. The thing about the Mentufacturer, he reflected, is that he can renew everything. He can abort the decay process by replacing the decaying object with a new one, one whose form is perfect. And then that decays. The Form Destroyer gets hold of it – and presently the Mentufacturer replaces that. As with a succession of old bees wearing out their wings, dying and being replaced at last by new bees. But I can't do that. I decay and the Form Destroyer has me. And it will get only worse.

God, he thought, help me.

But not by replacing me. That would be fine from a cosmological standpoint, but ceasing to exist is not what I'm after; and perhaps you understood this when you answered my prayer.

The scotch had made him sleepy; to his chagrin he found himself nodding. To bring himself back to full wakefulness: that was necessary. Leaping up he strode to his portable phonograph, took a visrecord at random, and placed it on the turntable. At once the far wall of the room lit up, and bright shapes intermingled with one another, a mixture of motion and of life, but unnaturally flat. He reflexively adjusted the depth-circuit; the figures began to become three dimensional. He turned up the sound as well.

'. . . Legolas is right. We may not shoot an old man so, at unawares and unchallenged, whatever fear or doubt be on us. Watch and wait!'

The bracing words of the old epic restored his perspective; he returned to his desk, reseated himself and got out the document which his supervisor had given him. Frowning, he studied the coded information, trying to decipher it. In numbers, punch-holes and letters it spelled out his new life, his world to come.

'. . . You speak as one that knows Fangorn well. Is that so?' The visrecord played on, but he no longer heard it; he had begun to get the gist of the encoded message.

'What have you to say that you did not say at our last meeting?' a sharp and powerful voice said. He glanced up and found himself confronted by the grey-clad figure of

Gandalf. It was as if Gandalf were speaking to him, to Ben Tallchief. Calling him to account. 'Or, perhaps, you have things to unsay?' Gandalf said.

Ben rose, went over to the phonograph and shut it off. I do not feel able at this time to answer you, Gandalf, he said to himself. There are things to be done, real things; I can't indulge myself in a mysterious, unreal conversation with a mythological character who probably never existed. The old values, for me, are suddenly gone; I have to work out what these damn punch-holes, letters and numbers mean.

He was beginning to get the drift of it. Carefully, he replaced the lid on the bottle of scotch, twisting it tight. He would go in a noser alone; at the colony he would join roughly a dozen others, recruited from a variety of sources. Range 5 of skills: a class C operation, on a K-4 pay scale. Maximum time: two years of operation. Full pension and medical benefits, starting as soon as he arrived. An override for any instructions he had already received, hence he could go at once. He did not have to terminate his work here before leaving.

And I have the three silver dollars for the noser, he said to himself. So that is that; nothing else to worry about. Except—

He could not discover what his job would consist of. The letters, numbers and punch-holes failed to say, or perhaps it was more correct to say that he could not get them to divulge this one piece of information – a piece he would much have wanted.

But it still looked good. I like it, he said to himself. I want it. Gandalf, he thought, I have nothing to unsay; prayers are not often answered and I will take this. Aloud he said, 'Gandalf, you no longer exist except in men's minds, and what I have here comes from the One, True and Living Deity, who is completely real. What more can I hope for?' The silence of the room confronted him; he did not see Gandalf now because he had shut the record off. 'Maybe someday,' he continued, 'I will unsay this. But not yet; not now. You understand?' He waited, experiencing the silence, knowing that he could begin it or end it by a mere touch of the phonograph's switch.

TWO

Seth Morley neatly divided the Gruyère cheese lying before him with a plastic-handled knife and said, 'I'm leaving.' He cut himself a giant wedge of cheese, lifted it to his lips via the knife. 'Late tomorrow night. Tekel Upharsin Kibbutz has seen the last of me.' He grinned, but Fred Gossim, the settlement's chief engineer, failed to return the message of triumph; instead Gossim frowned even more strongly. His disapproving presence pervaded the office.

Mary Morley said quietly, 'My husband applied for this transfer eight years ago. We never intended to stay here. You knew that.'

'And we're going with them,' Michael Niemand stammered in excitement. 'That's what you get for bringing a top-flight marine biologist here and then setting him to work hauling blocks of stone from the goddam quarry. We're sick of it.' He nudged his undersized wife, Clair. 'Isn't that right?'

'Since there is no body water on this planet,' Gossim said gratingly, 'we could hardly put a marine biologist to use in his stated profession.'

'But you advertised, eight years ago, for a marine biologist,' Mary Morley pointed out. This made Gossim scowl even more profoundly. 'The mistake was yours.'

'But,' Gossim said, 'this is your home. All of you—' He gestured at the group of kibbutz officials crowded around the entrance of the office. 'We all built this.'

'And the cheese,' Seth Morley said, 'is terrible, here. Those quakkip, those goat-like suborganisms that smell like the Form Destroyer's last year's underwear – I want very much to have seen the last of them and it. The quakkip and the cheese both.' He cut himself a second slice of the expensive, imported Gruyère cheese. To Niemand he said, 'You can't come with us. Our instructions are to make the flight by noser. Point A. A noser holds only two people; in this case my wife and me. Point B. You and your wife are two more people, *ergo* you won't fit. *Ergo* you can't come.'

'We'll take our own noser,' Niemand said.

'You have no instructions and/or permission to transfer to Delmak-O,' Seth Morley said from within his mouthful of cheese.

'You don't want us,' Niemand said.

'Nobody wants you,' Gossim grumbled. 'As far as I'm concerned without you we would do better. It's the Morleys that I don't want to see go down the drain.'

Eyeing him, Seth Morley said tartly, 'And this assignment is, *a priori* "down the drain." '

'It's some kind of experimental work,' Gossim said. 'As far as I can discern. On a small scale. Thirteen, fourteen people. It would be for you turning the clock back to the early days of Tekel Upharsin. You want to build up from that all over again? Look how long it's taken for us to get up to a hundred efficient, well-intentioned members. You mention the Form Destroyer. Aren't you by your actions decaying back the form of Tekel Upharsin?'

'And my own form too,' Morley said, half to himself. He felt grim, now; Gossim had gotten to him. Gossim had always been good with words, amazing in an engineer. It had been Gossim's silver-tongued words which had kept them all at their tasks throughout the years. But those words, to a good extent, had become vapid as far as the Morleys were concerned. The words did not work as they once had. And yet a glimmer of their past glory remained.

He could just not quite shake off the bulky, dark-eyed engineer.

But we're leaving, Morley thought. As in Goethe's *Faust*, 'In the beginning was the deed.' The deed and not the word, as Goethe, anticipating the twentieth century existentialists, had pointed out.

'You'll want to come back,' Gossim opined.

'Hmm,' Seth Morley said.

'And you know what I'll say to that?' Gossim said loudly. 'If I get a request from you – both of you Morleys – to come back here to Tekel Upharsin kibbutz, I'll say, "We don't have any need of a marine biologist; we don't even have an ocean. And we're not going to build so much as a puddle so that you can have a legitimate reason for working here.'

'I never asked for a puddle,' Morley said.

'But you'd like one.'

'I'd like *any* kind of body of water,' Morley said. 'That's the whole point; that's why we're leaving and that's why we won't be coming back.'

'You're sure Delmak-O has a body of water?' Gossim inquired.

'I assume—' Morley began, but Gossim cut him off.

'That,' Gossim said, 'is what you assumed about Tekel Upharsin. That's how your trouble began.'

'I assumed,' Morley said 'that if you advertised for a marine biologist—' He sighed feeling weary. There was no point trying to influence Gossim; the engineer – and chief officer of the kibbutz – had a closed mind. 'Just let me eat my cheese,' Morley said, and tried an additional slice. But he had grown tired of the taste; he had eaten too much. 'The hell with it,' he said, tossing his knife down. He felt irritable and he did not like Gossim; he felt no desire to continue the conversation. What mattered was the fact that no matter how he felt, Gossim could not revoke the transfer. It carried an override, and that was the long and the short of it . . . to quote William S. Gilbert

15

'I hate your bloody guts,' Gossim said.

Morley said, 'I hate yours, too.'

'A Mexican standoff,' Niemand said. 'You see, Mr Gossim, you can't make us stay; all you can do is yell.'

Making an obscene gesture towards Morley and Niemand Gossim strode off, parting the group gathered there, and disappeared somewhere on the far side. The office was quiet, now. Seth Morley immediately began to feel better.

'Arguments wear you out,' his wife said.

'Yes,' he agreed. 'And Gossim wears me out. I'm tired just from this one interchange, forgetting the eight full years of it which preceded today. I'm going to go select a noser.' He rose, made his way from the office and into the midday sun.

A noser is a strange craft, he said to himself as he stood at the edge of the parking field surveying the lines of inert vessels. First of all, they were incredibly cheap; he could gain possession of one of these for less than four silver dollars. Secondly, they could go but never return; nosers were strictly one-way ships. The reason, of course, was simple: a noser was too small to carry fuel for a return trip. All the noser could do was kick off from a larger ship or a planetary surface, head for its destination, and quietly expire there. But – they did their job. Sentient races, humans and otherwise, flocked throughout the galaxy aboard the little pod-like ships.

Goodbye, Tekel Upharsin, Morley said to himself, and made a brief, silent salute to the rows of orange bushes growing beyond the noser parking lot.

Which one should we take? he asked himself. They all looked alike: rusty, discarded. Like the contents of a used car lot back on Terra. I'll choose the first one with a name on it beginning with M, he decided, and began reading the individual names.

The *Morbid Chicken*. Well, that was it. Not very transcendental, but fitting; people, including Mary, were

16

always telling him that he had a morbid streak. What I have, he said to himself, is a mordant wit. People confuse the two terms because they sound similar.

Looking at his wristwatch he saw that he had time to make a trip to the packaging department of the citrus products factory. So he made off in that direction.

'Ten pint jars of class AA marmalade,' he said to the shipping clerk. It was either get them now or not at all.

'Are you sure you are entitled to ten more pints?' The clerk eyed him dubiously, having had dealings with him before.

'You can check on my marmalade standing with Joe Perser,' Morley said. 'Go ahead, pick up the phone and give him a call.'

'I'm too busy,' the clerk said. He counted out ten pint jars of the kibbutz's main product and passed them to Morley in a bag, rather than in a cardboard carton.

'No carton?' Morley said.

'Scram,' the clerk said.

Morley got one of the jars out, making sure that they were indeed class AA. They were. 'Marmalade from Tekel Upharsin Kibbutz!' the label declared. 'Made from genuine Seville oranges (group 3-B mutational subdivision). Take a pot of sunny Spain into your kitchen or cooking cubicle!' 'Fine,' Morley said. 'And thanks.' He lugged the bulky paper bag from the building and out once more into the bright sun of midday.

Back again at the noser parking area he began getting the pints of marmalade stored away in the *Morbid Chicken*. The one good thing this kibbutz produces, he said to himself as he placed the jars one by one within the magnetic grip-field of the storage compartment. I am afraid this is the one thing I'll miss.

He called Mary on his neck radio. 'I've picked out a noser,' he informed her. 'Come on down to the parking area and I'll show it to you.'

'Are you sure it's a good one?'

'You know you can take my mechanical ability for granted,' Morley said testily. 'I've examined the rocket engine, wiring, controls, every life-protect system, everything, completely.' He pushed the last jar of marmalade away in the storage area and shut the door firmly.

She arrived a few minutes later, slender and tanned in her khaki shirt, shorts and sandals. 'Well,' she said, surveying the *Morbid Chicken*, 'it looks rundown to me. But if you say it's okay it is, I guess.'

'I've already begun loading,' Morley said.

'With what?'

Opening the door of the storage compartment he showed her the ten jars of marmalade.

After a long pause Mary said, 'Christ.'

'What's the matter?'

'You haven't been checking the wiring and the engine. You've been out scrounging up all the goddam marmalade you could talk them out of.' She slammed the storage area door shut with venomous ire. 'Sometimes I think you're insane. Our lives depend on this goddam noser working. Suppose the oxygen system fails or the heat circuit fails or there're microscopic leaks in the hull. Or—'

'Get your brother to look at it,' he interrupted. 'Since you have so much more trust in him than you do in me.'

'He's busy. You know that.'

'Or he'd be here,' Morley said, 'picking out which noser for us to take. Rather than me.'

His wife eyed him intently, her spare body drawn up in a vigorous posture of defiance. Then, all at once, she sagged in what appeared to be half-amused resignation. 'The strange thing is,' she said, 'that you have such good luck – I mean in relation to your talents. This probably *is* the best noser here. But not because you can tell the difference but because of your mutant-like luck.'

'It's not luck. It's judgement.'

'No,' Mary said shaking her head. 'That's the last thing

it is. You have no judgement – not in the usual sense, any-how. But what the hell. We'll take this noser and hope your luck is holding as well as usual. But how can you live like this, Seth?' She gazed up plaintively into his face. 'It's not fair to me.'

'I've kept us going so far.'

'You've kept us here at this – kibbutz,' Mary said. 'For eight years.'

'But now I've gotten us off.'

'To something worse, probably. What do we know about this new assignment? Nothing, except what Gos-sim knows – and he knows because he makes it his business to read over everyone else's communications. He read your original prayer . . . I didn't want to tell you because I knew it would make you so—'

'That bastard.' He felt red, huge fury well up inside him, spiked with impotence. 'It's a moral violation to read another person's prayers.'

'He's in charge. He feels everything is his business. Any-how we'll be getting away from that. Thank God. Come on; cool off. You can't do anything about it; he read it years ago.'

'Did he say whether he thought it was a good prayer?'

Mary Morley said, 'Fred Gossim would never say if it was. I think it was. Evidently it was, because you got the transfer.'

'I think so. Because God doesn't grant too many prayers by Jews due to that covenant back in the pre-Intercessor days when the power of the Form Destroyer was so strong, and our relationship to him – to God, I mean – was so fouled up.'

'I can see you back in those days,' Mary said. 'Kvetching bitterly about everything the Mentufacturer did and said.'

Morley said, 'I would have been a great poet. Like David.'

'You would have held a little job, like you do now.' With

that she strode off, leaving him standing in the doorway of the noser, one hand on his row of stored-away marmalade jars.

His sense of impotence rose within him, choking his windpipe. 'Stay here!' he yelled after her. 'I'll leave without you!'

She continued on under the hot sun, not looking back and not answering.

For the remainder of the day Seth Morley busied himself loading their possessions into the *Morbid Chicken*. Mary did not show herself. He realized, towards dinner time, that he was doing it all. Where is she? he asked himself. It's not fair.

Depression hit him, as it generally did toward meal time. I wonder if it's all worth it, he said to himself. Going from one no-good job to another. I'm a loser. Mary is right about me; look at the job I did selecting a noser. Look at the job I'm doing loading this damn stuff in here. He gazed about the interior of the noser, conscious of the ungainly piles of clothing, books, records, kitchen appliances, typewriter, medical supplies, pictures, wear-forever couch covers, chess set, reference tapes, communications gear and junk, junk, junk. What have we in fact accumulated in eight years of work here? he asked himself. Nothing of any worth. And in addition, he could not get it all into the noser. Much would have to be thrown away or left for someone else to use. Better to destroy it, he thought gloomily. The idea of someone else gaining the use of his possessions had to be sternly rejected. I'll burn every last bit of it, he told himself. Including all the nebbish clothes that Mary's collected in her jaybird manner. Selecting whatever's bright and gaudy.

I'll pile her stuff outside, he decided, and then get all of mine aboard. It's her own fault: she should be here to help. I'm under no mandate to load her kipple.

As he stood there with an armload of clothes gripped

tightly he saw, in the gloom of twilight, a figure approaching him. Who is it? he wondered, and peered to see.

It was not Mary. A man, he saw, or rather something like a man. A figure in a loose robe, with long hair falling down his dark, full shoulders. Seth Morley felt fear. The Walker-on-Earth, he realized. Come to stop me. Shaking, he began to set down the armload of clothes. Within him his conscience bit furiously; he felt now the complete weight of all the bad-doings he had done. Months, years – he had not seen the Walker-on-Earth for a long time, and the weight was intolerable. The accumulation which always left its mark within. Which never departed until the Intercessor removed it.

The figure halted before him. 'Mr Morley,' it said.

'Yes,' he said, and felt his scalp bleeding perspiration. His face dripped with it and he tried to wipe it away with the back of his hand. 'I'm tired,' he said. 'I've been working for hours to get this noser loaded. It's a big job.'

The Walker-on-Earth said, 'Your noser, the *Morbid Chicken*, will not get you and your little family to Delmak-O. I therefore must interfere, my dear friend. Do you understand?'

'Sure,' he said, panting with guilt.

'Select another.'

'Yes,' he said, nodding frantically. 'Yes, I will. And thank you; thanks a lot. The fact of the matter is you saved our lives.' He peered at the dim face of the Walker-on-Earth, trying to see if its expression reproached him. But he could not tell; the remaining sunlight had begun to diffuse into an almost nocturnal haze.

'I am sorry,' the Walker-on-Earth said, 'that you had to labour so long for nothing.'

'Well, as I say—'

'I will help you with the reloading,' the Walker-on-Earth said. It reached its arms out, bending; it picked up a pile of boxes and began to move among the parked, silent nosers. 'I recommend this,' it said presently, halting by one and reaching to open its door. 'It's not much to look at, but mechanically it's perfect.'

'Hey,' Morley said, following with a swiftly snatched-up load. 'I mean, thanks. Looks aren't important anyhow; it's what's on the inside that counts. For people as well as nosers.' He laughed, but the sound emerged as a jarring screech; he cut if off instantly, and the sweat gathered around his neck turned cold with his great fear.

'There's no reason to be afraid of me,' the Walker said.

'Intellectually I know that,' Morley said.

Together, they laboured for a time in silence, carrying box after box from the *Morbid Chicken* to the better noser. Continually Morley tried to think of something to say, but he could not. His mind, because of his fright, had become dim; the fires of his quick intellect, in which he had so much faith, had almost flickered off.

'Have you ever thought of getting psychiatric help?' the Walker asked him at last.

'No,' he said.

'Let's pause a moment and rest. So we can talk a little.'

Morley said, 'No.'

'Why not?'

'I don't want to know anything; I don't want to hear anything.' He heard his voice bleat out in its weakness, steeped in its paucity of knowledge. The bleat of foolishness, of the greatest amount of insanity of which he was capable. He knew this, heard it and recognized it, and still he clung to it; he continued on. 'I know I'm not perfect,' he said. 'But I can't change. I'm satisfied.'

'Your failure to examine the *Morbid Chicken*.'

'Mary made a good point; usually my luck is good.'

'She would have died, too.'

'Tell her that.' Don't tell me, he thought. Please, don't tell me any more. I don't want to know!

The Walker regarded him for a moment. 'Is there anything,' it said at last, 'that you want to say to me?'

'I'm grateful, damn grateful. For your appearance.'

'Many times during the past years you've thought to yourself what you would say to me if you met me again. Many things passed through your mind.'

'I – forget,' he said, huskily.

'May I bless you?'

'Sure,' he said, his voice still husky. And almost inaudible. 'But why? What have I done?'

'I am proud of you, that's all.'

'But why?' He did not understand; the censure which he had been waiting for had not arrived.

The Walker said, 'Once years ago you had a tom cat whom you loved. He was greedy and mendacious and yet you loved him. One day he died from bone fragments lodged in his stomach, the result of filching the remains of a dead Martian root-buzzard from a garbage pail. You were sad, but you still loved him. His essence, his appetite – all that made him up had driven him to his death. You would have paid a great deal to have him alive again, but you would have wanted him as he was, greedy and pushy, himself as you loved him, unchanged. Do you understand?'

'I prayed then,' Morley said. 'But no help came. The Mentufacturer could have rolled time back and restored him.'

'Do you want him back now?'

'Yes,' Morley said raspingly.

'Will you get psychiatric help?'

'No.'

'I bless you,' the Walker-on-Earth said, and made a motion with his right hand: a slow and dignified gesture of blessing. Seth Morley bowed his head, pressed his right hand against his eyes . . . and found that black tears had lodged in the hollows of his face. Even now, he marvelled. That awful old cat; I should have forgotten him years ago. I guess you never really forget such things, he thought. It's all in there, in the mind, buried until something like this comes up.

'Thank you,' he said, when the blessing ended.

'You will see him again,' the Walker said. 'When you sit with us in Paradise.'

'Are you sure?'

'Yes.'

'Exactly as he was?'

'Yes.'

'Will he remember me?'

'He remembers you now. He waits. He will never stop waiting.'

'Thanks,' Morley said. 'I feel a lot better.'

The Walker-on-Earth departed.

Entering the cafeteria of the kibbutz, Seth Morley sought out his wife. He found her eating curried lamb shoulder at a table in the shadows of the edge of the room. She barely nodded as he seated himself facing her.

'You missed dinner,' she said presently. 'That's not like you.'

Morley said, 'I saw him.'

'Who?' She eyed him keenly.

'The Walker-on-Earth. He came to tell me that the noser I picked out would have killed us. We never would have made it.'

'I knew that,' Mary said. 'I knew that – *thing* would never have gotten us there.'

Morley said, 'My cat is still alive.'

'You don't have a cat.'

He grabbed her arm, halting her motions with the fork. 'He says we'll be all right; we'll get to Delmak-O and I can begin the new job.'

'Did you ask him what the new job is all about?'

'I didn't think to ask him that, no.'

'You fool.' She pried his hand loose and resumed eating. 'Tell me what the Walker looked like.'

'You've never seen it?'

'You *know* I've never seen it!'

24

'Beautiful and gentle. He held out his hand and blessed me.'

'So it manifested itself to you as a man. Interesting. If it had been as a woman you wouldn't have listened to—'

'I pity you,' Morley said. 'It's never intervened to save you. Maybe it doesn't consider you worth saving.'

Mary, savagely, threw down her fork; she glowered at him with animal ferocity. Neither of them spoke for a time.

'I'm going to Delmak-O alone,' Morley said at last.

'You think so? You really think so? I'm going with you; I want to keep my eyes on you at all times. Without me—'

'Okay,' he said scathingly. 'You can come along. What the hell do I care? Anyhow if you stayed here you'd be having an affair with Gossim, ruining his life—' He ceased speaking, panting for breath.

In silence, Mary continued eating her lamb.

THREE

'You are one thousand miles above the surface of Delmak-O,' the headphone clamped against Ben Tallchief's ear declared. 'Switch to automatic pilot, please.'

'I can land her myself,' Ben Tallchief said into his mike. He gazed at the world below him, wondering at its colours. Clouds, he decided. A natural atmosphere. Well, that answers one of my many questions. He felt relaxed and confident. And then he thought of his next question: Is this a god-world? And that issue sobered him.

He landed without difficulty . . . stretched, yawned, belched, unfastened his seat belt, stood up, awkwardly walked to the hatch, opened the hatch, then went back to the control room to shut off the still active rocket engine.

While he was at it he shut off the air supply, too. That seemed to be all. He clambered down the iron steps and bounced his way clumsily on to the surface of the planet.

Next to the field a row of flat-roofed buildings: the tiny colony's interwoven installations. Several persons were moving towards his noser, evidently to greet him. He waved, enjoying the feel of the plastic leather steering gloves – that and the very great augmentation of his somatic self which his bulky suit provided.

'Hi!' a female voice called.

'Hi,' Ben Tallchief said, regarding the girl. She wore a dark smock with matching pants, a general issue outfit that matched the plainness of her round, clean, freckled face. 'Is this a god-world?' he asked, walking leisurely toward her.

'It is not a god-world,' the girl said, 'but there are some strange things out there.' She gestured toward the horizon vaguely; smiling at him in a friendly manner she held out her hand. 'I'm Betty Jo Berm. Linguist. You're either Mr Tallchief or Mr Morley; everyone else is here already.'

'Tallchief,' he said.

'I'll introduce you to everyone. This elderly gentleman is Bert Kosler, our custodian.'

'Glad to meet you, Mr Kosler.' Handshake.

'I'm glad to meet you, too,' the old man said.

'This is Maggie Walsh, our theologian.'

'Glad to meet you, Miss Walsh.' Handshake. Pretty girl.

'Glad to meet you, too, Mr Tallchief.'

'Ignatz Thugg, thermoplastics.'

'Hi, there.' Overly masculine handshake. He did not like Mr Thugg.

'Dr Milton Babble, the colony's MD.'

'Nice to know you, Dr Babble.' Handshake. Babble, short and wide, wore a colourful short-sleeved shirt. His face had on it a corrupt expression which was hard to penetrate.

'Tony Dunkelwelt, our photographer and soil-sample expert.'

'Nice to meet you.' Handshake.

'This gentleman here is Wade Frazer, our psychologist.' A long, phony handshake with Frazer's wet, unclean fingers.

'Glen Belsnor, our electronics and computer man.'

'Glad to meet you.' Handshake. Dry, horny, competent hand.

A tall, elderly woman approached, supporting herself with a cane. She had a noble face, pale in its quality but very fine. 'Mr Tallchief,' she said, extending a slight, limp hand to Ben Tallchief. 'I am Roberta Rockingham, the sociologist. It's nice to meet you. We've all been wondering and wondering about you.'

Ben said, "Are you *the* Roberta Rockingham?' He felt himself glow with the pleasure of meeting her. Somehow he had assumed that the great old lady had died years ago. It confused him to find himself being introduced to her now.

'And this,' Betty Jo Berm said, 'is our clerk-typist, Susie Dumb.'

'Glad to know you, Miss—' He paused.

'Smart,' the girl said. Full-breasted and wonderfully shaped. 'Suzanne Smart. They think it's funny to call me Susie Dumb.' She extended her hand and they shook.

Betty Jo Berm said, 'Do you want to look around, or just what?'

Ben said, 'I'd like to know the purpose of the colony. They didn't tell me.'

'Mr Tallchief,' the great old sociologist said, 'they didn't tell us either.' She chuckled. 'We've asked everyone in turn as he arrives and no one knows. Mr Morley, the last man to arrive – he won't know either, and then where will we be?'

To Ben, the electronics maintenance man said, 'There's no problem. They put up a slave satellite; it's orbiting five times a day and at night you can see it go past. When the last person arrives – that'll be Morley – we're instructed to remote activate the audio tape transport aboard the satellite, and from the tape we'll get our instructions and an explanation of what we're doing and why we're here and all the rest of that crap; everything we want to know except "How do you make the refrig colder so the beer doesn't get warm?" Yeah, maybe they'll tell us that, too.'

A general conversation among the group of them was building up. Ben found himself drifting into it without really understanding it. 'At Betelgeuse 4 we had cucumbers, and we didn't grow them from moonbeams, the way you hear.' 'I've never seen him.' 'Well, he exists. You'll see him someday.' 'We've got a linguist so evidently there're sentient organisms here, but so far our expeditions have been informal, not scientific. That'll change when—' 'Nothing changes. Despite Specktowsky's theory of God entering history and starting time into motion again.' 'If you want to talk about that, talk to Miss Walsh. Theological matters don't interest me.' 'You can say that again. Mr Tallchief, are you part Indian?' 'Well, I'm about one-eighth Indian. You mean the name?' 'These buildings are built lousy. They're already ready to fall down. We can't get it warm when we need warm; we can't cool it when we need cool. You know what I think? I think this place was built to last only a very short time. Whatever the hell we're here for we won't be long; or rather, if we're here long we'll have to construct new installations, right down to the electrical wiring.' 'Some bug squeaks in the night. It'll keep you awake for the first day or so. By "day" of course I mean twenty-four-hour period. I don't mean "daylight" because it's not in the daytime that it squeaks, it's at night. Every goddam night. You'll see.' 'Listen, Tallchief, don't call Susie "dumb". If there's one thing she's not it's dumb.' 'Pretty, too.' 'And do you notice how her—' 'I noticed, but I don't think we should discuss it.' 'What line of work did you say you're in, Mr Tallchief? Pardon?' 'You'll have to speak up, she's a little deaf.' 'What I said was—' 'You're frightening her. Don't stand so close to her.' 'Can I get a cup of coffee?' 'Ask Maggie Walsh. She'll fix one for you.' 'If I can get the damn pot to shut off when it's hot; it's been just boiling the coffee over and over.' 'I don't see why our coffee pot won't work. They perfected them back in the twentieth century. What's left to know that we don't know already?' 'Think of it as being like Newton's colour theory. Everything about colour that could be known was known by 1800. And then Land came along with his two-light-scource and intensity theory, and what had seemed a closed field was busted all over.' 'You mean there may be things about self-regulating coffee pots that we don't know? That we just think we know?' 'Something like that.' And so on. He listened distantly, answered when he was spoken to and then, all at once fatigued, he wandered off, away from the group, toward a cluster of leathery green trees: they looked to Ben as if they constituted the primal source for the covering of psychiatrists' couches.

The air smelled bad – faintly bad – as if a waste-processing plant were chugging away in the vicinity. But in a couple of days I'll be used to it, he informed himself.

There is something strange about these people, he said to himself. What is it? They seem so . . . he hunted for the word. Overly bright. Yes, that was it. Prodigies of some sort, and all of them ready to talk. And then he thought, I think they're very nervous. That must be it; like me, they're here without knowing why. But – that didn't fully explain it. He gave up, then, and turned his attention outwards to embrace the pompous green-leather trees, the hazy sky overhead, the small nettle-like plants growing at his feet.

This is a dull place, he thought. He felt swift disappointment. Not much better than the ship; the magic had already left. But Betty Jo Berm had spoken of unusual life forms beyond the perimeter of the colony. So possibly he couldn't justifiably extrapolate on the basis of this little area. He would have to go deeper, farther and farther away from the colony. Which, he realized, is what they've all been doing. Because after all, what else is there to do? At least until we receive our instructions from the satellite.

I hope Morley gets here soon, he said to himself. So we can get started.

A bug crawled up on to his right shoe, paused there, and then extended a miniature television camera. The lens of the camera swung so that it pointed directly at his face.

'Hi,' he said to the bug.

Retracting its camera, the bug crawled off, evidently satisfied. I wonder who or what it's probing for? he wondered. He raised his foot, fooling momentarily with the idea of crushing the bug, and then decided not to. Instead he walked over to Betty Jo Berm and said, 'Were the monitoring bugs here when you arrived?'

'They began to show up after the buildings were erected. I think they're probably harmless.'

'But you can't be sure.'

'There isn't anything we can do about them anyhow. At first we killed them, but whoever made them just sent more out.'

'You better trace them back to their source and see what's involved.'

'Not "you," Mr Tallchief. "We." You're as much a part of this operation as anyone here. And you know just as much – and just as little – as we do. After we get our instructions we may find that the planners of this operation want us to – or do not want us to – investigate the indigenous life forms here. We'll see. But meanwhile, what about coffee?'

'You've been here how long?' Ben asked her as they sat at a plastic micro-bar sipping coffee from faintly grey plastic cups.

'Wade Frazer, our psychologist, arrived first. That was roughly two months ago. The rest of us have been arriving in dribs and drabs. I hope Morley comes soon. We're dying to hear what this is all about.'

'You're sure Wade Frazer doesn't know?'

'Pardon?' Betty Jo Berm blinked at him.

'He was the first one here. Waiting for the rest of you. I mean of us. Maybe this is a psychological experiment they've set up, and Frazer is running it. Without telling anyone.'

'What we're afraid of,' Betty Jo Berm said, 'is not that. We have one vast fear, and that is this: there is no purpose to us being here, and we'll never be able to leave. Everyone came here by noser: that was mandatory. Well, a noser can land but it can't take off. Without outside help we'd never be able to leave here. Maybe this is a prison – we've thought of that. Maybe we've all done something, or anyhow someone *thinks* we've done something.' She eyed him alertly with her grey, calm eyes. 'Have you done anything, Mr Tallchief?' she asked.

'Well, you know how it is.'

'I mean, you're not a criminal or anything.'

'Not that I know of.'

'You look ordinary.'

'Thanks.'

'I mean, you don't look like a criminal.' She rose, walked across the cramped room to a cupboard. 'How about some Seagram's VO?' she asked.

'Fine,' he said, pleased at the idea.

As they sat drinking coffee laced with Seagram's VO Canadian whisky (imported) Dr Milton Babble strolled in, perceived them, and seated himself at the bar. 'This is a second-rate planet,' he said to Ben without preamble. His dingy, shovel-like face twisted in distaste. 'It just plain is second rate. Thanks.' He accepted his cup of coffee from Betty Jo, sipped, still showed distaste. 'What's in this?' he demanded. He then saw the bottle of Seagram's VO. 'Hell, that ruins coffee,' he said angrily. He set his cup down again, his expression of distaste greater than ever.

'I think it helps,' Betty Jo Berm said.

Dr Babble said, 'You know, it's a funny thing, all of us here together. Now see, Tallchief, I've been here a month and I have yet to find someone I can talk to, really talk to. Every person here is completely involved with himself and doesn't give a damn about the others. Excluding you, of course, B.J.'

Betty Jo said, 'I'm not offended. It's true. I don't care about you, Babble, or any of the rest. I just want to be left alone.' She turned toward Ben. 'We have an initial curiosity when someone lands . . . as we had about you. But afterward, after we see the person and listen to him a little—' She lifted her cigarette from the ashtray and inhaled its smoke silently. 'No offence meant, Mr Tallchief, as Babble just now said. We'll get you pretty soon and you'll be the same; I predict it. You'll talk with us for a while and then you'll withdraw into—' She hesitated, groping the air with her right hand as if physically searching for a word. As if a word were a three dimensional object which she could seize manually. 'Take Belsnor. All he thinks about is the refrigeration unit. He has a phobia that it'll stop working, which you would gather from his panic would mean the end of us. He thinks the refrigeration unit is keeping us from—' She gestured with her cigarette. 'Boiling away.'

'But he's harmless,' Dr Babble said.

'Oh, we're all harmless,' Betty Jo Berm said. To Ben she said, 'Do you know what I do, Mr Tallchief? I take pills. I'll show you.' She opened her purse and brought out a pharmacy bottle. 'Look at these,' she said as she handed the bottle to Ben. 'The blue ones are stelazine, which I use as an anti-emetic. You understand: I use it for that, but that isn't its basic purpose. Basically stelazine is a tranquillizer, in doses of less than twenty milligrams a day. In greater doses it's an anti-hallucinogenic agent. But I don't take it for that either. Now, the problem with stelazine is that it's a vasodilator. I sometimes have trouble standing up after I've taken some. Hypostasis, I think it's called.'

Babble grunted, 'So she also takes a vasoconstrictor.'

'That's this little white tablet,' Betty Jo said, showing him the part of the bottle in which the white tablets dwelt. 'It's methamphetamine. Now, this green capsule is—'

'One day,' Babble said, 'your pills are going to hatch, and some strange birds are going to emerge.'

'What an odd thing to say,' Betty Jo said.

'I meant they look like coloured birds' eggs.'

'Yes, I realize that. But it's still a strange thing to say.' Removing the lid from the bottle she poured out a variety of pills into the palm of her hand. 'This red cap – that's of course pentabarbital, for sleeping. And then this yellow one, it's norpramin, which counterbalances the CNS depressive effect of the mellaril. Now, this square orange tab, it's new. It has five layers on it which time-release on the so-called "trickle principle". A very effective CNS stimulant. Then a—'

'She takes a central nervous system depressor,' Babble broke in, 'and also a CNS stimulant.'

Ben said, 'Wouldn't they cancel each other out?'

'One might say so, yes,' Babble said.

'But they don't,' Betty Jo said. 'I mean subjectively I can feel the difference. I know they're helping me.'

'She reads the literature on them all,' Babble said. 'She brought a copy of the *PDR* with her – *Physicians' Desk Reference* – with lists of side effects, contra-indications, dosage, when indicated and so forth. She knows as much about her pills as I do. In fact, as much as the manufacturers know. If you show her a pill, any pill, she can tell you what it is, what it does, what—' He belched, drew himself up higher in his chair, laughed, and then said, 'I remember a pill that had as side effects – if you took an overdose – convulsions, coma and then death. And in the literature, right after it told about the convulsions, coma and death, it said, "May Be Habit Forming". Which always struck me as an anticlimax.' Again he laughed, and then pried at his nose with one hairy, dark finger. 'It's a strange world,' he murmured. 'Very strange.'

Ben had a little more of the Seagram's VO. It had begun to fill him with a familiar warm glow. He felt himself beginning to ignore Dr Babble and Betty Jo. He sank into the privacy of his own mind, his own being, and it was a good feeling.

Tony Dunkelwelt, photographer and soil-sample specialist, put his head in the door and called. 'There's another noser landing. It must be Morley.' The screen door banged shut as Dunkelwelt scuttled off.

Half-rising to her feet, Betty Jo said, 'We'd better go. So at last, we're finally all here.' Dr Babble rose, too. 'Come on, Babble,' she said and started toward the door. 'And you, Mr Eighth-Part-Indian-Tallchief.'

Ben drank down the rest of his coffee and Seagram's VO and got up dizzily. A moment later and he was following them out the door and into the light of day.

FOUR

Shutting off the retrojets Seth Morley shuddered, then unfastened his seat belt. Pointing, he instructed Mary to do the same.

'I know,' Mary said, 'what to do. You don't have to treat me like a child.'

'You're sore at me,' Morley said, 'even though I navigated us here perfectly. The whole way.'

'You were on automatic pilot and you followed the beam,' she said archly. 'But you're right, I should be grateful.' Her tone of voice did not sound grateful, however. But he did not care. He had other things on his mind.

He manually unbolted the hatch. Green sunlight

streamed in and he saw, shielding his eyes, a barren landscape of meagre trees and even more meagre brush. Off to the left a gaggle of unimpressive buildings jutted irregularly. The colony.

People were approaching the noser, a gang of them. Some of them waved and he waved back. 'Hello,' he said, stepping down the iron pins and dropping to the ground. Turning, he began to help Mary out but she shook him loose and descended without assistance.

'Hi,' a plain, brownish girl called as she approached. 'We're glad to see you – you're the last!'

'I'm Seth Morley,' he said. 'And this is Mary, my wife.'

'We know,' the plain, brownish girl said, nodding. 'Glad to meet you. I'll introduce you to everyone.' She indicated a muscular youth nearby. 'Ignatz Thugg.'

'Glad to meet you.' Morley shook hands with him. 'I'm Seth Morley and this is my wife Mary.'

'I'm Betty Jo Berm,' the plain, brownish girl said. 'And this gentleman—' She directed his attention toward an elderly man with a stooped, fatigue posture. 'Bert Kosler, our custodian.'

'Glad to meet you, Mr Kosler.' Vigorous handshake.

'I'm glad to meet you, too, Mr Morley. And Mrs Morley. I hope you will enjoy it here.'

'Our photographer and soil-sample expert, Tony Dunkelwelt.' Miss Berm pointed out a long-snouted teenager who glared sullenly and did not extend his hand.

'Hello,' Seth Morley said to him.

''Lo.' The boy glowered down at his own feet.

'Maggie Walsh, our specialist in theology.'

'Glad to meet you, Miss Walsh.' Vigorous handshake. What a really nice-looking woman, Morley thought to himself. And here came another attractive woman, this one wearing a sweater stretched tight over her peek-n-squeeze bra. 'What's your field?' he asked her as they shook hands.

'Clerical work and typing. My name is Suzanne.'

35

'What's your last name?'

'Smart.'

'That's a nice name.'

'I don't think so. They call me Susie Dumb, which isn't really all that funny.'

'I don't think it's funny at all,' Seth Morley said.

His wife nudged him violently in the ribs and, being well-trained, he at once cut his conversation with Miss Smart short and turned to greet a skinny, rat-eyed individual who held out a wedge-shaped hand which appeared to have sharpened, tapered edges. He felt an involuntary refusal arise within him. This was not a hand he wanted to shake, and not a person he wanted to know.

'Wade Frazer,' the rat-eyed individual said. 'I'm acting as the settlement's psychologist. By the way – I've done an introductory TAT test on everyone as they've arrived. I'd like to do one on both of you, possibly later today.'

'Sure,' Seth Morley said, without conviction.

'This gentleman,' Miss Berm said, 'is our doctor, Milton G. Babble of Alpha 5. Say hello to Dr Babble, Mr Morley.'

'Glad to meet you, doctor.' Morley shook hands.

'You're a bit overweight, Mr Morley,' Dr Babble said.

'Hmm,' Morley said.

An elderly woman, extremely tall and straight, came out of the group, moving with the aid of a cane. 'Mr Morley,' she said, and extended a light limp hand to Seth Morley. 'I am Roberta Rockingham the sociologist. It's a pleasure to meet you, and I do hope you had a pleasurable voyage here with not too much trouble.'

'We did fine.' Morley accepted her little hand and delicately shook it. She must be 110 years old, by the look of her, he said to himself. How can she function still? How did she get here? He could not picture her piloting a noser across interplanetary space.

'What is the purpose of this colony?' Mary asked.

'We'll find out in a couple of hours,' Miss Berm said. 'As soon as Glen – Glen Belsnor, our electronics and computer expert – is able to raise the slave satellite orbiting this planet.'

'You mean you don't know?' Seth Morley said. 'They never told you?'

'No, Mr Morley,' Mrs Rockingham said in her deep, elderly voice. 'But we'll know now and we've waited so long. It'll be such a delight to know why all of us are here. Don't you think so, Mr Morley? I mean, wouldn't it be wonderful for all of us to know our purpose?'

'Yes,' he said.

'So you do agree with me, Mr Morley. Oh, I think that's so nice that we can all agree.' To Seth Morley she said in a low, meaningful voice, 'That's the difficulty, I'm afraid Mr Morley. We have no common purpose. Interpersonal activity has been at a low ebb but of course it will pick up, now that we can—' She bent her head to cough briefly into a diminutive handkerchief. 'Well it really is so nice,' she finished at last.

'I don't agree,' Frazer said. 'My preliminary testing indicates that by and large this is an inherently ego-oriented group. As a whole, Morley, they show what appears to be an innate tendency to avoid responsibility. It's hard for me to see why some of them were chosen.'

A grimy, tough-looking individual in work clothes said, 'I notice you don't say "us". You say "they".'

'Us, they.' The psychologist gestured convulsively. 'You show obsessive traits. That's another overall unusual statistic for this group: you're all hyper-obsessive.'

'I don't think so,' the grimy individual said in a level but firm voice. 'I think what it is is that you're nuts. Giving those tests all the time has warped your mind.'

That started all of them talking. Anarchy had broke out. Going up to Miss Berm, Seth Morley said, 'Who's in charge of this colony? You?' He had to repeat it twice before she heard.

'No one has been designated,' she answered loudly, over the noise of the group quarrel. 'That's one of our problems. That's one of the things we want to—' Her voice trailed off in the general din.

'At Betelgeuse 4 we had cucumbers, and we didn't grow them from moonbeams, the way you hear. For one thing, Betelgeuse 4 has no moon, so that should answer that.' 'I've never seen him. And I hope I never will.' 'You'll see him someday.' 'The fact that we have a linguist on our staff suggests that there're sentient organisms here, but so far we don't know anything because our expeditions have been informal, sort of like picnics, not in any way scientific. Of course, that'll change when—' 'Nothing changes. Despite Specktowsky's theory of God entering history and starting time into motion again.' 'No, you've got that wrong. The whole struggle before the Intercessor came took place in time, a very long time. It's just that everything has happened so fast since then, and it's so relatively easy, now in the Specktowsky Period, to directly contact one of the Manifestations. That's why in a sense our time is different from even the first two thousand years since the Intercessor first appeared.' 'If you want to talk about that, talk to Maggie Walsh. Theological matters don't interest me.' 'You can say that again. Mr Morley, have you ever had contact with any of the Manifestations?' 'Yes, as a matter of fact I have. Just the other day – I guess it was Wednesday by Tekel Upharsin time – the Walker-on-Earth approached me to inform me that I had been given a faulty noser, the result of the using of which would have cost my wife and I our lives.' 'So it saved you. Well, you must be very pleased to know that it would intercede for you that way. It must be a wonderful feeling.' 'These buildings are built lousy. They're already ready to fall down. We can't get it warm when we need warm; we can't cool it when we need cool. You know what I think? I think this place was built to last only a very short time. Whatever the hell we're here for we won't be long; or rather, if we're here long we'll have to construct new installations, right down to the BX cable.' 'Some insect or plant squeaks in the night. It'll keep you awake for the first day or so, Mr and Mrs Morley. Yes, I'm trying to speak to you, but it's hard with all the noise. By "day" of course I mean the twenty-four-hour period. I don't mean "daytime" because it's not in the daytime that it squeaks. You'll see.' 'Hey Morley, don't get like the others and start calling Susie "dumb". If there's one thing she's not it's dumb.' 'Pretty, too.' 'And do you notice how her—' 'I noticed, but – my wife, you see. She takes a dim view so perhaps we'd better drop the subject.' 'Okay, if you say so. What field are you in, Mr Morley?' 'I'm a qualified marine biologist.' 'Pardon? Oh, were you speaking to me, Mr Morley? I can't quite make it out. If you could say it again.' 'Yeah, you'll have to speak up. She's a little deaf.' 'What I said was—' 'You're frightening her. Don't stand so close to her.' 'Can I get a cup of coffee or a glass of milk anywhere?' 'Ask Maggie Walsh, she'll fix one for you. Or B.J. Berm.' 'Oh Christ, if I can just get the damn pot to shut off when it's hot. It's been just boiling the coffee over and over again.' 'I don't see why our communal coffee pot won't work, they perfected them back in the early part of the twentieth century. What's left to know that we don't know?' 'Think of it as being like Newton's Colour Theory. Everything about colour that could be known was known by 1800.' 'Yes, you always bring that up. You're obsessive about it.' 'And then Land came along with his two-light source and intensity theory, and what had seemed a closed field was busted into pieces.' 'You mean there may be things about homeostatic coffee pots that we don't know? That we just think we know?' 'Something along that order.' And so on.

Seth Morley groaned. He moved away from the group, toward a tumble of great water-smoothed rocks. A body of water had been here at some time, anyhow. Although perhaps by now it was entirely gone.

The grimy, lanky individual in work clothes broke away from the group and followed after him. 'Glen Belsnor,' he said, extending his hand.

'Seth Morley.'

'We're a friggin' mob, Morley. It's been like this since I got here, right after Frazer came.' Belsnor spat into nearby weeds. 'You know what Frazer tried to do? Since he was the first one here he tried to set himself up as the group-leader; he even told us – told me, for example – that he "Understood his instructions to mean that he would be in charge." We almost believed him. It sort of made sense. He was the first one to arrive and he started giving those frig-gin' tests to everybody and then making loud comments about our "statistical abnormalities", as the creep puts it.'

'A competent psychologist, a reliable one, would never make a public statement of his findings.' A man not yet introduced to Seth Morley came walking up, hand ex-tended. He appeared to be in his early forties, with a slightly large jaw, ridged brows, and shiny black hair. 'I'm Ben Tallchief,' he informed Morley. 'I arrived just before you did.' He seemed to Seth Morley to be a little unsteady; as if, Morley reflected, he'd had a drink or three. He put out his hand and they shook. I like this man, he thought to himself. Even if he has had a couple. He has a different aura from the others. But, he thought, maybe they were all right before they got here, and something here made them change.

If that is so, he thought, it will change us, too, Tallchief, Mary and I. Eventually.

The thought did not please him.

'Seth Morley here,' he said. 'Marine biologist, formerly attached to the staff of Tekel Upharsin Kibbutz. And your field is—'

Tallchief said, 'I am a qualified naturalist, class B. Aboard ship there was little to do, and it was a ten year flight. So I prayed, via the ship's transmitter, and the relay picked it up and carried it to the Intercessor. Or perhaps it was the Mentufacturer. But I think the former, because there was no rollback of time.'

'It's interesting to hear that you're here because of a

prayer,' Seth Morley said. 'In my case I was visited by the Walker-on-Earth at the time in which I was busy finding an adequate noser for the trip here. I picked one out, but it wasn't adequate; the Walker said it would never have gotten Mary and myself here.' He felt hungry. 'Can we get a meal pried loose from this outfit?' he asked Tallchief. 'We haven't eaten today; I've been busy piloting the noser for the last twenty-six hours. I only picked up the beam at the end.'

Glen Belsnor said, 'Maggie Walsh will be glad to slap together what passes as a meal around here. Something along the lines of frozen peas, frozen ersatz veal steak, and coffee from the goddam unhomeostatic friggin' coffee machine, which never worked even at the start. Will that do?'

'It will have to,' Morley said, feeling gloom.

'The magic departs fast,' Ben Tallchief said.

'Pardon?'

'The magic of this place.' Tallchief made a sweeping gesture which took in the rocks, the gnarly green trees, the wobble of low hut-like buildings which made up the colony's sole installations. 'As you can see.'

'Don't sell it completely short,' Belsnor spoke up. 'These aren't the only structures on this planet.'

'You mean there's a native civilization here?' Morley asked, interested.

'I mean there're things out there that we don't understand. There is a building. I've caught a glimpse of it, one time on the prowl, and I was going back but I couldn't find it again. A big grey building – really big – with turrets, windows, I would guess about eight floors high. I'm not the only one who's seen it,' he added defensively. 'Berm saw it; Walsh saw it; Frazer says he saw it, but he's probably horse-crudding us. He just doesn't want to look like he's left out.'

Morley said, 'Was the building inhabited?'

'I couldn't tell. We couldn't see that much from where

we were; none of us really got that close. It was very—'
He gestured. 'Forbidding.'

'I'd like to see it,' Tallchief said.

'Nobody's leaving the compound today,' Belsnor said.
'Because now we can contact the satellite and get our instructions. And that comes first; that's what really matters.'
He spat into the weeds once more, deliberately and
thoughtfully. And with accurate aim.

Dr Milton Babble examined his wristwatch and thought,
It's four-thirty and I'm tired. Low blood sugar, he decided.
It's always a sign of that when you get tired in the late
afternoon. I should try to get some glucose into myself
before it becomes serious. The brain, he thought, simply
can't function without adequate blood sugar. Maybe, he
thought, I'm becoming diabetic. That could be; I have the
right genetic history

'What's the matter, Babble?' Maggie Walsh said, seated
beside him in the austere briefing hall of their meagre
settlement. 'Sick again?' She winked at him, which at once
made him furious. 'What's it now? Are you wasting away,
like Camille, from TB?'

'Hypoglycemia,' he said, studying his hand as it rested
on the arm of his chair. 'Plus a certain amount of extra-
pyramidal neuromuscular activity. Motor restlessness of
the dystonic type. Very uncomfortable.' He hated the sen-
sation: his thumb twitching in the familiar pellet-rolling
motion, his tongue curling up within his mouth, dryness
in his throat – dear God, he thought, is there no end of
this?

Anyhow the herpes simplex keratitis which had afflicted
him during the previous week had abated. He was glad of
that (thank God).

'Your body is to you like what a house is for a woman,'
Maggie Walsh said. 'You keep experiencing it as if it were
an environment, rather than—'

'The somatic environment is one of the realest environments in which we live,' Babble said testily. 'It's our first environment, as infants, and then as we decline into old age, and the Form Destroyer corrodes our vitality and shape, we once again discover that it little matters what goes on in the so-called outside world when our somatic essence is in jeopardy.'

'Is this why you became a doctor?'

'It's more complex than a simple cause-and-effect relationship. That supposes a duality. My choice of vocations—'

'Pipe down over there,' Glen Belsnor yapped, pausing in his fiddlings. Before him rested the settlement's transmitter, and he had been trying for several hours to get it functioning. 'If you want to talk clear out.' Several other people in the hall added noisy agreement.

'Babble,' Ignatz Thugg said from the seat in which he sprawled, 'you're well-named.' He barked a canine-like laugh.

'You, too,' Tony Dunkelwelt said to Thugg.

'Pipe down!' Glen Belsnor yelled, his face red and steaming as he poked the innards of the transmitter. 'Or by God we'll never get our poop-sheet from the friggin' satellite. If you don't shut up I'm going to come over there and take you apart instead of taking this mass of metallic guts apart. And I'd enjoy it.'

Babble rose, turned and left the hall.

In the cold, long sunlight of late afternoon he stood smoking his pipe (being careful not to start up any pyloric activity) and contemplated their situation. Our lives, he thought, are in the hands of little men like Belsnor; here, they rule. The kingdom of the one-eyed, he thought acidly, in which the blind are king. What a life.

Why did I come here? he asked himself. No answer immediately came, only a wail of confusion from within him: drifting shapes that complained and cried out like indignant patients in a charity ward. The shrill shapes plucked at him, drawing him back into the world of for-

43

mer times, into the restlessness of his last years on Orionus 17, back to the days with Margo, the last of his office nurses with whom he had conducted a long, inelegant affair, a misadventure which had ended up in a heap of tangled tragi-comedy – both for him and for her. In the end she had left him . . . or had she? Actually, he reflected, everyone leaves everyone when something is as messy and jury-rigged as that terminates. I was lucky, he thought, to get out of it how and when I did. She could have made a lot more trouble. As it was, she had seriously jeopardized his physical health, just by protein depletion alone.

That's right, he thought. It's time for my wheat germ oil my vitamin E. Must go to my quarters. And, while I'm there, I'll take a few glucose tablets to counterbalance my hypoglycemia. Assuming I don't pass out on the way. And if I did, who would care? What in fact would they do? I'm essential to their survival, whether they recognize it or not. I'm vital to them, but are they vital to me? Yes, in the sense that Glen Belsnor is; vital because they can do, or allegedly can do, skilled tasks necessary for the maintenance of this stupid little incestuous small town that we're running here. This pseudo-family that doesn't work as a family in any respect. Thanks to the meddlers from outside.

I'm going to have to tell Tallchief and – what's his name? Morley. Tell Tallchief and Morley and Morley's wife – who is not bad-looking at all – about the meddlers from outside, about the building which I have seen . . . seen close enough to read the writing above the entrance. Which no one else has. Insofar as I know.

He started down the gravel path towards his quarters. As he came up on to the plastic porch of the living quarters he saw four people in a gathering together: Susie Smart, Maggie Walsh, Tallchief and Mr Morley. Morley was talking, his tub-shaped middle protruding like a huge inguinal hernia. I wonder what he lives on, Babble said to himself. Potatoes, broiled steak, with ketchup on everything, and beer. You can always tell a beer drinker. They have that

44

perforated facial skin, perforated where the hairs grow, and the bags under their eyes. They look, as he looks, as if they have an œdema puffing them out. And renal damage as well. And of course the ruddy skin.

A self-indulgent man, he thought, like Morley, doesn't in any way understand – *can't* understand – that he's pouring poisons into his body. Minute embolisms . . . damage to critical areas of the brain. And yet they keep on, these oral types. Regression to a pre-reality testing stage. Maybe it's a misplaced biological survival mechanism: for the good of the species they weed themselves out. Leaving the women to more competent, and more advanced male types.

He walked up to the four of them, stood with his hands in his pockets, listening. Morley was relating the minutiae of a theological experience which he evidently had had. Or pretended to have had.

'. . . "my dear friend," he called me. Obviously I mattered to him. He helped me with the reloading . . . it took a long time and we talked. His voice was low but I could understand him perfectly. He never used any excess words and he could express himself perfectly; there was no mystery about it, like you sometimes hear. Anyhow, we loaded and talked. And he wanted to bless me. Why? Because – he said – I was exactly the kind of person who mattered to him. He was completely matter-of-fact about it; he simply stated it. "You are the kind of person whom I think matters," he said, or words to that effect. "I'm proud of you," he said. "Your great love of animals, your compassion toward lower life forms, pervades your entire mentality. Compassion is the basis of the person who has risen from the confines of the Curse. A personality type like yours is exactly what we are looking for".' Morley paused then.

'Go on,' Maggie Walsh said, in a fascinated voice.

'And then he said a strange thing,' Morley said. 'He said, "As I have saved you, saved your life, by my own compassion, I know that your own great capacity for compassion will enable you to save lives, both physically and spiritually, of others." Presumably he meant here at Delmak-O.'

'But he didn't say,' Susie Smart said.

'He didn't have to,' Morley said. 'I knew what he meant; I understood everything he said. In fact I could communicate a lot more clearly with him than with most of the people I've known. I don't mean any of you – hell, I don't really know you, yet – but you see what I mean. There weren't any transcendental symbolic passages, no metaphysical nonsense like they used to talk about before Specktowsky wrote The Book. Specktowsky was right; I can verify it on the basis of my own experiences with him. With the Walker.'

'Then you've seen it before,' Maggie Walsh said.

'Several times.'

Dr Milton Babble opened his mouth and said, 'I've seen it seven times. And I encountered the Mentufacturer once. So if you add it together I've had eight experiences with the One True Deity.'

The four of them gazed at him with various expressions. Susie Smart looked sceptical; Maggie Walsh showed absolute disbelief; both Tallchief and Morley seemed relatively interested.

'And twice,' Babble said, 'with the Intercessor. So it's ten experiences in all. Throughout my whole life, of course.'

'From what you heard from Mr Morley about his experience,' Tallchief said, 'did it sound similar to your own?'

Babble kicked at a pebble on the porch; it bounced away, struck the near-by wall, fell silent, then. 'Fairly much so. By and large. Yes, I think we can in some part accept what Morley says. And yet—' He hesitated meaningfully. 'I'm afraid I'm sceptical. Was it truly the Walker, Mr Morley? Could it not have been a passing itinerant labourer who wanted you to think he was the Walker? Had you thought of that? Oh, I'm not denying that the Walker appears again and again among us; my own experiences testify to that.'

46

'I know he was,' Morley said, looking angry, 'because of what he said about my cat.'

'Ah, your cat.' Babble smiled both within and without; he felt deep and hearty amusement transverse his circulatory system. 'So this is where the business about your 'great compassion for lower life forms" comes from.'

Looking nettled and even more angrily outraged Morley said, 'How would a passing tramp know about my cat? Anyhow, there aren't any passing tramps at Tekel Upharsin. Everybody works; that's what a kibbutz is.' He looked, now, hurt and unhappy.

The voice of Glen Belsnor dinned in the darkened distance behind them. 'Come on in! I've made contact with the goddam satellite! I'm about to have it run its audio tapes!'

Babble, as he started walking, said, 'I didn't think he could do it.' How good he felt, although he did not know exactly why. Something to do with Morley and his awe-inspiring account of meeting the Walker. Which now did not seem awe-inspiring after all. Once it had been scrupulously investigated and by a person with adult, critical judgement.

The five of them entered the briefing hall and seated themselves among the others. From the speakers of Belsnor's radio equipment sharp static punctuated with random voice-noises sounded. The din hurt Babble's ears, but he said nothing. He displayed the formal attention which the technician had demanded.

'What we're picking up right now is a scatter track,' Belsnor informed them over the racket. 'The tape hasn't started to run yet; it won't do that until I give the satellite the right signal.'

'Start the tape,' Wade Frazer said.

'Yeah, Glen, start the tape.' Voices from here and there in the chamber.

'Okay,' Belsnor said. He reached out, touched control knobs on the panel before him. Lights winked on and off as servo-assisted mechanisms switched into activity aboard the satellite.

From the speakers a voice said, 'Greetings to the Delmak-O colony from General Treaton of Interplan West.'

'That's it,' Belsnor said. 'That's the tape.'

'Shut up, Belsnor. We're listening.'

'It can be run back any number of times,' Belsnor said.

'You have now completed your recruiting.' General Treaton of Interplan West said. 'This completion was anticipated by us at Interplan RAV to occur not later than the fourteenth of September, Terran statute time. First, I would like to explain why the Delmak-O colony was created, by whom and for what purpose. It is basically—' All at once the voice stopped. 'Wheeeeee,' the speakers blared. 'Ughhhhhhh. Akkkkkkkkk.' Belsnor stared at the receiving gear with mute dismay. 'Ubbbbb,' the speakers said; static burst in, receded as Belsnor twisted dials, and then — silence.

After a pause Ignatz Thugg guffawed.

'What is it, Glen?' Tony Dunkelwelt said.

Belsnor said thickly, 'There are only two tape-heads used in transmitters such as are aboard the satellite. An erase head, mounted first on the transport, then a replay-record head. What has happened is that the replay-record head has switched from replay to record. So it is erasing the tape an inch ahead automatically. There's no way I can switch it off; it's on record and that's where it'll probably stay. Until the whole tape is erased.'

'But if it erases,' Wade Frazer said, 'then it'll be gone forever. No matter what you do.'

'That's right,' Glen Belsnor said. 'It's erasing and then recording nothing. I can't get it out of the record mode. Look.' He snapped several switches open and shut. 'Nothing. The head is jammed. So much for that.' He slammed a major relay into place, cursed, sat back, removed his glasses and wiped his forehead 'Christ,' he said. 'Well so it goes.'

The speakers twittered briefly with cross talk, then fell silent again. No one in the room spoke. There was nothing to say.

FIVE

'What we can do,' Glen Belsnor said, 'is to transmit to the relay network, transmit so it'll be carried back to Terra, and inform General Treaton at Interplan West of what's happened, that our briefing of his instructions has failed to take place. Under the circumstances they'll undoubtedly be willing – and able – to fire off a communications rocket in our direction. Containing a second tape which we can run through the transport here.' He pointed to the tape deck mounted within the radio gear.

'How long will that take?' Susie Smart asked.

'I haven't ever tried to raise the relay network from here,' Glen Belsnor said. 'I don't know; we'll have to see. Maybe we can do it right away. But at the most it shouldn't take more than two or three days. The only problem would be—' He rubbed his bristly chin. 'There may be a security factor. Treaton may not want this request run through the relay network, where anyone with a class one receiver can pick it up. His reaction then would be to ignore our request.'

'If they do that,' Babble spoke up, 'we ought to pack up and leave here. Immediately.'

'Leave how?' Ignatz Thugg said, grinning.

Nosers, Seth Morley thought. We have no vehicles here except inert and fuel-zero nosers, and even if we could round up the fuel – say by siphoning from every fuel tank to fill up one – they don't have tracking gear by which we could pilot a course. They would have to use Delmak-O

49

as one of two coordinates, and Delmak-O is not on Inter-plan West charts – hence no tracking value. He thought, Is this why they insisted on our coming in nosers?

They're experimenting with us, he thought wildly. That's what this is: an experiment. Maybe there never were any instructions on the satellite's tape. Maybe it all was planned.

'Make a sample try at picking up the relay people.' Tall-chief said. 'Maybe you can get them right now.'

'Why not?' Belsnor said. He adjusted dials, clamped an earphone to the side of his head, opened circuits, closed others down. In absolute silence the others waited and watched. As if, Morley thought, our lives depended on this. And – perhaps they do.

'Anything?' Betty Jo Berm asked at last.

Belsnor said, 'Nothing. I'll switch it on video.' The small screen jumped into life. Mere lines, visual static. 'This is the frequency on which the relay operates. We should pick them up.'

'But we're not,' Babble said.

'No. We're not.' Belsnor continued to spin dials. 'It's not like the old days,' he said, 'when you could tinker with a variable condenser until you got your signal. This is complex.' All at once he shut off the central power supply; the screen blacked out and, from the speakers, snatches of static ceased.

'What's the matter?' Mary Morley asked.

'We're not on the air,' Belsnor said.

'What?' Startled exclamations from virtually all of them.

'We're not transmitting. I can't pull them and if we're not on the air they sure as hell aren't going to pull us.' He leaned back, convulsed with disgust. 'It's a plot, a friggin' plot.'

'You mean that literally?' Wade Frazer demanded. 'You mean this is intentional?'

'I didn't assemble our transmitter,' Glen Belsnor said. 'I didn't hook up our receiving equipment. For the last month, since I've been here, in fact, I've been making sample tests; I've picked up several transmissions from operators in this star system, and I was able to transmit back. Everything seemed to be working normally. And then this.' He stared down, his face working. 'Oh,' he said abruptly. He nodded. 'Yes, I understand what happened.'

'Is it bad?' Ben Tallchief asked.

Belsnor said, 'When the satellite received my signal to activate the audio tape construct and complying transmitter, the satellite sent a signal back. A signal to this gear.' He indicated the receiver and transmitter rising up before him. 'The signal shut down everything. It overrode my instructions. We ain't receiving and we ain't transmitting, no matter what I tell this junk to do. It's off the air, and it'll probably take another signal from the satellite to get it functioning again.' He shook his head. 'What can you do but admire it?' he said. 'We transmit our initial instruction to the satellite; in response it sends one back. It's like chess: move and respond. I started the whole thing going. Like a rat in a cage, trying to find the lever that drops food. Rather than the one that transmits an electric shock.' His voice was bitter, and laden with defeat.

'Dismantle the transmitter and receiver,' Seth Morley said. 'Override the override by removing it.'

'It probably – hell, undoubtedly – has a destruct component in it. It's either already destroyed vital elements or it will when I try to search for it. I have no spare parts; if it's destroyed a circuit here and there I can't do anything towards fixing it.'

"The automatic pilot beam,' Morley said, 'that I followed to get here. You can send out the message on it.'

'Automatic pilot beams work for the first eighty or ninety thousands miles and then peter out. Isn't that where you picked up yours?'

'More or less,' he admitted.

'We're totally isolated,' Belsnor said. 'And it was done in a matter of minutes.

'What we must do,' Maggie Walsh said, 'is to prepare a

joint prayer. We can probably get through on pineal gland emanation, if we make it short.'

'I can help on preparing it, if that's the criterion,' Betty Jo Berm said. 'Since I'm a trained linguist.'

'As a last resort,' Belsnor said.

'Not as a last resort,' Maggie Walsh said. 'As an effective, proven method of getting help. Mr Tallchief, for example, got here because of a prayer.'

'But it passed along the relay,' Belsnor said. 'We have no way to reach the relay.'

'You have no faith in prayer?' Wade Frazer asked, nastily.

Belsnor said, 'I have no faith in prayer that's not electronically augmented. Even Specktowsky admitted that; if a prayer is to be effective it must be electronically transmitted through the network of god-worlds so that all Manifestations are reached.'

'I suggest,' Morley said, 'that we transmit our joint prayer as far as we can through the automatic pilot beam. If we can project it eighty or ninety thousands miles out it should be easier for the Deity to pick it up ... since gravity works in inverse proportion to the power of the prayer, meaning that if you can get the prayer away from a planetary body – and ninety thousand miles is reasonably away – then there is a good mathematical chance of the various Manifestations receiving it, and Specktowsky mentions this; I forget where. At the end, I think, in one of his addenda.'

Wade Frazer said, 'It's against Terran law to doubt the power of prayer. A violation of the civil code of all Interplan West stages and holdings.'

'And you'd report it,' Ignatz Thugg said.

'Nobody's doubting the efficacy of prayer,' Ben Tallchief said, eyeing Frazer with overt hostility. 'We're merely disagreeing on the most effective way of handling it.' He got to his feet. 'I need a drink,' he said. 'Goodbye.' He left the room, tottering a little as he went.

'A good idea,' Susie Smart said to Seth Morley. 'I think I'll go along, too.' She rose, smiling at him in an automatic way, a smile devoid of feeling. 'This is really terrible, isn't it? I can't believe that General Treaton could have authorized this deliberately; it must be a mistake. An electronic breakdown that they don't know about. Don't you agree?'

'General Treaton from all I've heard,' Morley said, 'is a thoroughly reputable man.' Actually, he had never heard of General Treaton before, but it seemed to him a good thing to say, in order to try to cheer her up. They all needed cheering up, and if it helped to believe that General Treaton was definitely reputable then so be it; he was all for it. Faith in secular matters, as well as in theological matters, was a necessity. Without it one could not go on living.

To Maggie Walsh, Dr Babble said, 'Which aspect of the Deity should we pray to?'

'If you want time rolled back, say to the moment before any of us accepted this assignment,' Maggie said, 'then it would be to the Mentufacturer. If we want the Deity to stand in for us, collectively to replace us in this situation, then it would be the Intercessor. If we individually want help in finding our way out—'

'All three,' Bert Kosler said in a shaking voice. 'Let the Deity decide which part of himself he wishes to use.'

'He may not want to use any,' Susie Smart said tartly. 'We'd better decide on our own. Isn't that part of the art of praying?'

'Yes,' Maggie Walsh said.

'Somebody write this down,' Wade Frazer said. 'We should start by saying, "Thank you for all the help you have given us in the past. We hesitate to bother you again, what with all you have to do all the time, but our situation is as follows".' He paused, reflecting. 'What is our situation?' he asked Belsnor. 'Do we just want the transmitter fixed?'

'More than that,' Babble said. 'We want to get entirely out of here, and never have to see Delmak-O again.'

'If the transmitter's working,' Belsnor said, 'we can do that ourselves.' He gnawed on a knuckle of his right hand. 'I think we ought to settle for getting replacement parts for the transmitter and do the rest on our own. The less asked for in a prayer the better. Doesn't The Book say that?' He turned toward Maggie Walsh.

'On page 158,' Maggie said, 'Specktowsky says, "The soul of brevity – the short time we are alive – is wit. And as regards the art of prayer, wit runs inversely proportional to length".'

Belsnor said, 'Let's simply say, "Walker-on-Earth, help us find spare transmitter parts".'

'The thing to do,' Maggie Walsh said, 'is to ask Mr Tallchief to word the prayer, inasmuch as he was so successful in his recent previous prayer. Evidently he knows how to phrase properly.'

'Get Tallchief,' Babble said. 'He's probably moving his possessions from his noser to his living quarters. Somebody go find him.'

'I'll go,' Seth Morley said. He rose, made his way out of the briefing chamber and into the evening darkness.

'That was a very good idea, Maggie,' he heard Babble saying, and other voices joined his. A chorus of agreement went up from those gathered in the briefing room.

He continued on, feeling his way cautiously; it would be so easy to get lost in this still unfamiliar colony site. Maybe I should have let one of the others go, he said to himself. A light shone in the window of a building ahead. Maybe he's in there, Seth Morley said to himself, and made his way towards the light.

Ben Tallchief finished his drink, yawned, picked at a place on his throat, yawned once again and clumsily rose to his feet. Time to start moving, he said to himself. I hope, he thought, I can find my noser in the dark.

He stepped outdoors, found the gravel path with his feet, began moving in the direction which he supposed the nosers to be. Why no guide lights around here? he asked himself, and then realized that the other colonists had been too preoccupied to turn the lights on. The breakdown of the transmitter had ensnared the attention of every one of them, and justly so. Why aren't I in there? he asked himself. Functioning as part of the group. But the group didn't function as a group anyhow; it was always a finite number of self-oriented individuals squalling with one another. With such a bunch he felt as if he had no roots, no common source. He felt nomadic and in need of exercise; right now something called to him: it had called him from the briefing room and back to his living quarters, and now it sent him trudging through the dark, searching for his noser.

A vague area of darkness moved ahead of him, and, against the less-dark sky, a figure appeared. 'Tallchief?'

'Yes,' he said. 'Who is it?' He peered.

'Morley. They sent me to find you. They want you to compose the prayer, since you had such good luck a couple of days ago.'

'No more prayers for me,' Tallchief said, and clamped his teeth in bitterness. 'Look where that last prayer got me – stuck here with all of you. No offence, I just mean—' He gestured. 'It was a cruel and inhuman act to grant that prayer, considering the situation here. And it must have known it.'

'I can understand your feeling,' Morley said.

'Why don't you do it? You just recently met the Walker; it would be smarter to use you.'

'I'm no good at prayers. I didn't summon the Walker; it was his idea to come to me.'

'How about a drink?' Tallchief said. 'And then maybe you could give me a hand with my stuff, moving it to my quarters and like that.'

'I have to move my own stuff.'

'That's an outstanding cooperative attitude.'

'If you had helped me—'

Tallchief said, 'I'll see you later.' He continued on, groping and flailing in the darkness, until all at once he stumbled against a clanking hull. A noser. He had found the right area; now to pick out his own ship.

He looked back. Morley had gone; he was alone.

Why couldn't the guy have helped me? he asked himself. I'm going to need another person for most of the cartons. Let's see, he pondered. If I can turn on the landing lights of the noser I'll be able to see. He located the locking wheel of the hatch, spun it, tugged the hatch open. Automatically the safety lights came on; now he could see. Maybe I'll just move in my clothes, bathroom articles and my copy of The Book, he decided. I'll read The Book until I get ready to go to sleep. I'm tired; piloting the noser here took everything out of me. That and the transmitter failing. Utter defeat.

Why did I ask him to help me? he wondered. I don't know him, he hardly knows me. Getting my stuff moved is my own problem. He has problems of his own.

He picked up a carton of books, began to lug it away from the parked noser in the general direction – he hoped – of his living quarters. I've got to get a flashlight, he decided as he waddled along. And hell, I forgot to turn on the landing lights. This is all going wrong, he realized. I might as well go back and join the others. Or I could move this one carton and then have another drink, and possibly by that time most of them would have come out of the briefing room and could help me. Grunting and perspiring, he made his way up the gravel path toward the dark and inert structure which provided them with their living quarters. No lights on. Everyone was still involved in pasting together an adequate prayer. Thinking about that he had to laugh. They'll probably haggle about it all night, he decided, and laughed again, this time with angry disgust.

He found his own living quarters, by virtue of the fact that the door hung open. Entering, he dropped the carton of books to the floor, sighed, stood up, turned on all the lights . . . standing there he surveyed the small room with its dresser and bed. The bed did not please him; it looked small and hard 'Christ' he said, and seated himself on it. Lifting several books from the carton he rummaged about until he came onto the bottle of Peter Dawson scotch; he unscrewed the lid and drank sombrely from the bottle itself.

Through the open door he gazed out at the nocturnal sky; he saw the stars haze over with atmospheric disturbances, then clear for a moment. It is certainly hard, he thought to make out stars through the refractions of a planetary atmosphere.

A great grey shape merged with the doorway, blotting out the stars.

It held a tube and it pointed the tube at him. He saw a telescopic sight on it and a trigger mechanism. Who was it? What was it? He strained to see, and then he heard a faint pop. The grey shape receded and once more stars appeared. But now they had changed. He saw two stars collapse against one another and a nova form; it flared up and then, as he watched, it began to die out. He saw it turn from a furiously blazing ring into a dim core of dead iron and then he saw it cool into darkness. More stars cooled with it; he saw the force of the entropy, the method of the Destroyer of Forms, retract the stars into dull reddish coals and then into dust-like silence. A shroud of thermal energy hung uniformly over the world, over this strange and little world for which he had no love or use.

It's dying, he realized. The universe. The thermal haze spread on and on until it became only a disturbance, nothing more; the sky glowed weakly with it and then flickered. Even the uniform thermal disbursement was expiring. How strange and goddam awful he thought. He got to his feet, moved a step towards the door.

And there, on his feet, he died.

*   *   *

They found him an hour later. Seth Morley stood with his wife at the far end of the knot of people jammed into the small room and said to himself, *To keep him from helping with the prayer.*

'The same force that shut down the transmitter,' Ignatz Thugg said. 'They knew; they knew if he phrased the prayer it would go through. Even without the relay.' He looked grey and frightened. All of them did, Seth Morley noticed. Their faces in the light of the room, had a leaden, stone-like cast. Like, he thought, thousand-year-old idols.

Time, he thought, is shutting down around us. It is as if the future is gone, for all of us. Not just for Tallchief.

'Babble, can you do an autopsy?' Betty Jo Berm asked.

'To a certain extent.' Dr Babble had seated himself beside Tallchief's body and was touching him here and there. 'No visible blood. No sign of an injury. His death could be natural, you all realize; it might be that he had a cardiac condition. Or, for example he might have been killed by a heat gun at close range . . . but then, if that's the case, I'll find the burn marks.' He unfastened Tallchief's collar, reached down to explore the chest area. 'Or one of us might have done it,' he said. 'Don't rule that out.'

'They did it,' Maggie Walsh said.

'Possibly,' Babble said. 'I'll do what I can.' He nodded to Thugg and Wade Frazer and Glen Belsnor. 'Help me carry him into the clinic; I'll start the autopsy now.'

'None of us even knew him,' Mary said.

'I think I probably saw him last,' Seth Morley said. 'He wanted to bring his things from his noser here to his living area. I told him I'd help him later on, when I had time. He seemed to be in a bad mood; I tried to tell him we needed him to compose a prayer but he didn't seem interested. He just wanted to move his things.' He felt acutely guilty. Maybe if I had helped him he'd still be alive, he said to himself. Maybe Babble's right; maybe it was a heart attack, brought on by moving heavy cartons. He kicked at the box of books, wondering if this box had done it – this box and

58

his own refusal to help. Even when I was asked I wouldn't give it, he realized.

'You didn't see any indication of a suicidal attitude at work, did you?' Dr Babble asked.

'No.'

'Very strange,' Babble said. He shook his head wearily. 'Okay, let's get him to the infirmary.'

SIX

The four men carried Tallchief's body across the dark, nocturnal compound. Cold wind licked at them and they shivered; they drew together against the hostile presence of Delmak-O – the hostile presence which had killed Ben Tallchief.

Babble switched on lights here and there. At last they had Tallchief up on the high, metal-topped table.

'I think we should retire to our individual living quarters and stay there until Dr Babble has finished his autopsy,' Susie Smart said, shivering.

Wade Frazer spoke up. 'Better if we stayed together, at least until Dr Babble's report is in. And I also think that under these unexpected circumstances, this terrible event in our lives, that, we must immediately elect a leader, a strong one who can keep us together as a group, when in fact right now we are not, but should be – must be. Doesn't everyone agree?'

After a pause Glen Belsnor said, 'Yeah.'

'We can vote,' Betty Jo Berm said. 'In a democratic way. But I think we must be careful.' She struggled to express herself. 'We mustn't give a leader too much power. And we should be able to recall him when and if at any time we're not satisfied with him; then we can vote him out as our leader and elect someone else. But while he is leader we should obey him – we don't want him to be too weak, either. If he's too weak we'll just be like we are now: a mere collection of individuals who can't function together, even in the face of death.'

'Then let's get back to the briefing room,' Tony Dunkelwelt said, 'rather than to our personal quarters. So we can start casting votes. I mean, it or they could kill us before we have a leader; we don't want to wait.'

In a group they made their way sombrely from Dr Babble's infirmary to the briefing room. The transmitter and receiver were still on; each person, entering, heard the dull, low hum.

'So big,' Maggie Walsh said, gazing at the transmitter. 'And so useless.'

'Do you think we should arm ourselves?' Bert Kosler said, plucking at Morley's sleeve. 'If there's someone after us to kill all of us—'

'Let's wait for Babble's autopsy report,' Seth Morley said.

Seating himself, Wade Frazer said in a business-like way, 'We'll vote by a show of hands. Everybody sit down and be quiet and I'll read our names and keep the tally. Is that satisfactory to everyone?' There was a sardonic undertone to his voice, and Seth Morley did not like it.

Ignatz Thugg said, 'You won't get it, Frazer. No matter how badly you want it. Nobody in this room is going to let somebody like you tell them what to do.' He dropped into a chair, crossed his legs, and got a tobacco cigarette from his jacket pocket.

As Wade Frazer read off the names and took the tally, several others made their own notations. They don't trust Frazer to make an accurate account, Seth Morley realized. He did not blame them.

'The greatest number of votes for one person,' Frazer said, when all the names had been read, 'goes to Glen Belsnor.' He dropped his tally sheet with a blatant sneer ... as if, Morley thought, the psychologist is saying Go ahead and doom yourselves. It's your lives, if you want to toss them away. But it seemed to him that Belsnor was a good choice; on his own very limited knowledge he had himself voted for the electronics maintenance man. He was satisfied, even if Frazer was not. And by their relieved stir he guessed that most of the others were, too.

'While we're waiting for Dr Babble's report,' Maggie Walsh said, 'perhaps we should join in a group prayer for Mr Tallchief's psyche to be taken immediately into immortality.'

'Read from Specktowsky's Book,' Betty Jo Berm said. She dipped into her pocket and brought out her own copy, which she passed to Maggie Walsh. 'Read the part on page 70 about the Intercessor. Isn't it the Intercessor that we want to reach?'

From memory, Maggie Walsh intoned the words which all of them knew. ' "By His appearance in history and creation, the Intercessor offered Himself as a sacrifice by which the Curse could be partially nullified. Satisfied as to the redemption of His creation by this manifestation of Himself, this signal of His great – but partial – victory, the Deity 'died' and then remanifested Himself to indicate that He had overcome the Curse and hence death, and, having done this, moved up through the concentric circles back to God Himself." And I will add another part which is pertinent. "The next – and last – period is the Day of Audit, in which the heavens will roll back like a scroll and each living thing – and hence all creatures, both sentient man and man-like nonterrestrial organisms – will be reconciled with the original Deity, from whose unity of being everything has come (with the possible exception of the Form Destroyer)".' She paused a moment and then said, 'Repeat what I say after me, all of you, either aloud or in your thoughts.'

They lifted their faces and gazed straight upward, in the

accepted fashion. So that the Deity could hear them more readily.

'We did not know Mr Tallchief too well.'

They all said, 'We did not know Mr Tallchief too well.'

'But he seemed to be a fine man.'

They all said, 'But he seemed to be a fine man.'

Maggie hesitated, reflected, then said, 'Remove him from time and thereby make him immortal.'

'Remove him from time and thereby make him immortal.'

'Restore his form to that which he possessed before the Form Destroyer went to work on him.'

They all said, 'Restore his form to that—' They broke off. Dr Milton Babble had come into the briefing room, looking ruffled.

'We must finish the prayer,' Maggie said.

'You can finish it some other time,' Dr Babble said. 'I've been able to determine the cause of death.' He consulted several sheets of paper which he had brought along. 'Cause of death: vast inflammation of the bronchial passages, due to an unnatural amount of histamine in the blood, resulting in a stricture of the trachea; exact cause of death was suffocation as reaction to a heterogenic allergen. He must have been stung by an insect or brushed against a plant while he was unloading his noser. An insect or plant containing a substance to which he was violently allergic. Remember how sick Susie Smart was her first week here, from brushing against one of the nettle-like bushes? And Kosler.' He gestured in the direction of the elderly custodian. 'If he hadn't gotten to me as quick as he did he would be dead, too. With Tallchief the situation was against us; he had gone out by himself at night, and there was no one around to react to his plight. He died alone, but if we had been there he could have been saved.'

After a pause Roberta Rockingham, seated, with a huge rug over her lap, said, 'Why, I think that's ever so much more encouraging than our own speculation. It would appear that no one is trying to kill us . . . which is really quite wonderful, don't you think?' She gazed around at them, straining to hear if any had spoken.

'Evidently,' Wade Frazer said remotely, with a private grimace.

'Babble,' Ignatz Thugg said, 'we voted without you.'

'Good grief,' Betty Jo Berm said. 'That's so. We'll have to vote again.'

'You selected one of us as a leader?' Babble said. 'Without letting me exercise my own personal involvement? Who did you decide on?'

'On me,' Glen Belsnor said.

Babble consulted with himself. 'It's all right as far as I'm concerned,' he said at last, 'to have Glen as our leader.'

'He won by three votes,' Susie Smart said.

Babble nodded. 'In any case I'm satisfied.'

Seth Morley walked over to Babble, faced him and said, 'You're sure that was the cause of death?'

'Beyond doubt. I have equipment which can determine —'

'Did you find an insect bite-mark on him anywhere?'

'Actually no,' Babble said.

'A possible spot where a plant leaf might have speared him?'

'No,' Babble said, 'but that isn't an important aspect of such a determination. Some of the insects here are so small that any sting-spot or bite-spot wouldn't be visible without a microscopic examination, and that would take days.'

'But you're satisfied,' Belsnor said, also coming up; he stood with his arms folded, rocking back and forth on his heels.

'Absolutely.' Babble nodded vigorously.

'You know what it would mean if you're wrong.'

'How? Explain.'

'Oh Christ, Babble,' Susie Smart said, 'it's obvious. If someone or something deliberately killed him then we're

63

in just as much danger as he was – possibly. But if an insect stung him—'

'That's what it was,' Babble said. 'An insect stung him.' His ears had turned bright carmen with stubborn, irritable anger. 'Do you think this is my first autopsy? That I'm not capable of handling pathology-report instrumentation that I've handled all my adult life?' He glared at Susie Smart. 'Miss Dumb,' he said.

'Come on, Babble,' Tony Dunkelwelt said.

'It's Dr Babble to you, sonny,' Babble said.

Nothing is changed, Seth Morley said to himself. We are as we were, a mob of twelve people. And it may destroy us. End forever our various separate lives.

'I feel a vast amount of relief,' Susie Smart said, coming up beside him and Mary. 'I guess we were becoming paranoid; we thought everyone was after us, trying to kill us.'

Thinking about Ben Tallchief – and his last encounter with him – Morley felt no sympathetic resonance within him to her newly refreshed attitude. 'A man is dead,' he said.

'We barely knew him. In fact we didn't know him at all.'

'True,' Morley said. Maybe it's because I feel so much personal guilt. 'Maybe I did it,' he said aloud to her.

'A bug did it,' Mary said.

'May we finish the prayer, now?' Maggie Walsh said.

Seth Morley said to her, 'How come we need to shoot a petition-prayer eighty thousand miles up from the planet's surface, but this sort of prayer can be done without electronic help?' I know the answer, he said to himself. This prayer now – it really doesn't matter to us if it's heard. It is merely a ceremony, this prayer. The other one was different. The other time we needed something for ourselves, not for Tallchief. Thinking this he felt more gloomy than ever. 'I'll see you later,' he said aloud to Mary. 'I'm going to unpack the boxes I've brought from our noser.'

'But don't go near the nosers,' Mary warned him. 'Until

tomorrow; until we have time to scout out the plant or bug—'

'I won't be outdoors,' Morley agreed. 'I'll go directly to our quarters.' He strode from the briefing room out into the compound. A moment later he was ascending the steps to the porch of their joint living quarters.

I'll ask The Book, Seth Morley said to himself. He rummaged through several cartons and at last found his copy of *How I Rose From the Dead in My Spare Time and So Can You.* Seated, he held it on his lap, placed both hands on it, shut his eyes, turned his face upward and said, 'Who or what killed Ben Tallchief?'

He then, eyes shut, opened the book to a page at random, put his finger at one exact spot, and opened his eyes.

His finger rested on: the Form Destroyer.

That doesn't tell us much, he reflected. All death comes as a result of a deterioration of form, due to the activity of the Form Destroyer.

And yet it scared him.

It doesn't sound like a bug or a plant, he thought starkly. It sounds like something entirely else.

A tap-tap sounded at his door.

Rising warily, he moved by slow degrees to the door; keeping it shut he swept the curtain back from the small window and peered out into the night darkness. Someone stood on the porch, someone small, with long hair, tight sweater, peek-n-squeeze bra, tight short skirt, barefoot. Susie Smart has come to visit, he said to himself, and unlocked the door.

'Hi,' she said brightly, smiling up at him. 'May I come in and talk a little?'

He led her over to The Book. 'I asked it what or who killed Tallchief.'

'What did it say?' She seated herself, crossed her bare legs and leaned forward to see as he placed his finger on the same spot as before. 'The Form Destroyer,' she said soberly. 'But it's always the Form Destroyer.'

'Yet I think it means something.'

'That it wasn't an insect?'

He nodded.

'Do you have anything to eat or drink?' Susie said. 'Any candy?'

'The Form Destroyer,' he said, 'is loose outside.'

'You're scaring me.'

'Yes,' he said. 'I want to. We've got to get a prayer off this planet and to the relay network. We're not going to survive unless we get help.'

'The Walker comes without prayer,' Susie said.

'I have a Baby Ruth candy bar,' he said. 'You can have that.' He rummaged through a suitcase of Mary's, found it, handed it to her.

'Thank you,' she said, tearing the paper from one of the candy bar's blunt ends.

He said, 'I think we're doomed.'

'We're always doomed. It's the essence of life.'

'Doomed immediately. Not abstractly – doomed in the sense that I and Mary were doomed when I tried to load up the *Morbid Chicken. Mors certa, hora incerta;* there's a big difference between knowing that you're going to die and knowing you're going to die within the next calendar month.'

'Your wife is very attractive.'

He sighed.

'How long have you two been married?' Susie gazed at him intently.

'Eight years,' he said.

Susie Smart swiftly stood up. 'Come over to my place and let me show you how nice these little rooms can be fixed up. Come on – it's depressing in here.' She tugged little-girl-wise at his hand and he found himself following after her.

They danced up the porch, passed several doorways and

66

came at last to Susie's door. It was unlocked; she opened it, welcoming him into the warmth and light. She had told the truth; it did look nice. Can we make ours as nice as this? he asked himself as he looked around, at the pictures on the walls, the textures of fabrics, and the many, many planter boxes and pots, out of which multicoloured blossoms dazzled the eye.

'Nice,' he said.

Susie banged the door shut. 'Is that all you can say? It's taken me a month to make it look like this.'

' "Nice" was your word for it, not mine.'

She laughed. 'I can call it "nice", but since you're a visitor you have to be more lavish about it.'

'Okay,' he said, 'it's wonderful.'

'That's better.' She seated herself in a black canvas-backed chair facing him, leaned back, rubbed her hands together briskly, then fastened her attention on him. 'I'm waiting,' she said.

'For what?'

'For you to proposition me.'

'Why would I do that?'

Susie said, 'I'm the settlement whore. You're supposed to die of priapism because of me. Haven't you heard?'

'I just got here late today,' he pointed out.

'But somebody must have told you.'

'When somebody does,' he said, 'he'll get his nose punched in.'

'But it's true.'

'Why?' he said.

'Dr Babble explained to me that it's a diencephalic disturbance in my brain.'

He said, 'That Babble. You know what he said about my visit with the Walker? He said most of what I said was untrue.'

'Dr Babble has a keen little maliciousness about him. He loves to put down everyone and everything.'

'If you know that about him,' Seth Morley said, 'then you know enough not to pay any attention.'

'He just explained *why* I'm that way. I am that way. I've slept with every man in the settlement, except that Wade Frazer.' She shook her head, making a wry face. 'He's awful.'

With curiosity, he said, 'What does Frazer say about you? After all, he's a psychologist. Or claims he is.'

'He says that—' She reflected, staring up pensively at the ceiling of the room, meantime chewing abstractedly on her lower lip. 'It's a search for the great world-father archetype. That's what Jung would have said. Do you know about Jung?'

'Yes,' he said, although in fact he had only heard little more than the name; Jung, he had been told, had in many ways laid the groundwork for a *rapprochement* between intellectuals and religion – but at that point Seth Morley's knowledge gave out. 'I see,' he said.

'Jung believes that our attitudes toward our actual mothers and fathers are because they embody certain male and female archetypes. For instance, there's the great bad earth-father and the good earth-father and the destroying earth-father, and so forth . . . and the same with women. My mother was the bad earth-mother, so all my psychic energy was turned toward my father.'

'Hmm,' he said. He had, all at once, begun to think about Mary. Not that he was afraid of her, but what would she think when she got back to their living quarters and found him gone? And then – God forbid – found him here with Susie Dumb, the self-admitted settlement whore?

Susie said, 'Do you think the sexual act makes a person impure?'

'Sometimes,' he responded reflexively, still thinking about his wife. His heart laboured and he felt his pulse race. 'Specktowsky isn't too clear about that in The Book,' he mumbled.

'You're going to take a walk with me,' Susie said.

'Now? I am? Where? Why?'

'Not now. Tomorrow when it's daylight. I'll take you outside the settlement, out into the real Delmak-O. Where the strange things are, the movements that you catch out of the corner of your eye – and the Building.'

'I'd like to see the Building,' he said, truthfully.

Abruptly she rose. 'Better get back to your living quarters, Mr Seth Morley,' she said.

'Why?' He, too, confused, rose to his feet.

'Because if you stay here your attractive wife is going to find us and create chaos and open the way for the Form Destroyer, who you say is loose outside, to get all of us.' She laughed, showing perfect, pale teeth.

'Can Mary come on our walk?' he asked.

'No,' she shook her head. 'Just you. Okay?'

He hesitated, a flock of thoughts invading his mind; they pulled him this way and that, then departed, leaving him free to make an answer. 'If I can work it,' he said.

'Try. Please. I can show you all the places and life forms and things I've discovered.'

'Are they beautiful?'

'S-some. Why are you looking at me so intently? You make me nervous.'

'I think you're insane,' he said.

'I'm just outspoken. I simply say, "A man is a sperm's way of producing another sperm." That's merely practical.'

Seth Morley said, 'I don't know much about Jungian analysis, but I certainly do not recall—' He broke off. Something had moved at the periphery of his vision.

'What's the matter?' Susie Smart asked.

He turned swiftly, and this time saw it clearly. On the top of the dresser a small grey square object inched its way forward, then, apparently aware of him, ceased moving.

In two steps he was over to it; he snatched up the object, held it gripped tightly in the palm of his hand.

'Don't hurt it,' Susie said. 'It's harmless. Here, give it to

69

me.' She held out her hand, and, reluctantly, he opened his enclosing fingers.

The object which he held resembled a tiny building.

'Yes,' Susie said, seeing the expression on his face. 'It comes from the Building. It's a sort of offspring, I suppose. Anyhow it's exactly like the Building but smaller.' She took it from him, for a time examined it, then placed it back on the dresser. 'It's alive,' she said.

'I know,' he said. Holding it, he had felt the animate quality of it; it had pushed against his fingers, trying to get out.

'They're all over the place,' Susie said. 'Out there.' She made a vague gesture. 'Maybe tomorrow we can find you one.'

'I don't want one,' he said.

'You will when you've been here long enough.'

'Why?'

'I guess they're company. Something to break the monotony. I remember as a child finding a Ganymedian toad in our garden. It was so beautiful with its shining flame and its long smooth hair that—'

Morley said, 'It could have been one of these things that killed Tallchief.'

'Glen Belsnor took one apart one day,' Susie said. 'He said—' She pondered. 'It's harmless, anyhow. The rest of what he said was electronic talk; we couldn't follow it.'

'And he'd know?'

'Yes.' She nodded.

Seth Morley said, 'You – we – have a good leader.' But I don't think quite good enough, he said to himself.

'Shall we go to bed?' Susie said.

'What?' he said.

'I'm interested in going to bed with you. I can't judge a man unless I've been in bed with him.'

'What about women?'

'I can't judge them at all. What, do you think I go to bed with the women, too? That's depraved. That sounds like something Maggie Walsh would do. She's a lesbian, you know. Or didn't you know?'

'I don't see that it matters. Or that it's any of our business.' He felt shaky and uneasy. 'Susie,' he said, 'you should get psychiatric help.' He remembered, all at once, what the Walker-on-Earth had said to him, back at Tekel Upharsin. Maybe we all need psychiatric help, he thought. But not from Wade Frazer. That's totally, entirely out.

'You don't want to go to bed with me? You'd enjoy it, despite your initial prudery and reservations. I'm very good. I know a lot of ways. Some which you probably never heard about. I made them up myself.'

'From years of experience,' he said.

'Yes.' She nodded. 'I started at twelve.'

'No,' he said.

'Yes,' Susie said, and grabbed him by the hand. On her face he saw a desperate expression, as if she were fighting for her life. She drew him towards her, straining with all her strength; he held back and she strained vainly.

Susie Smart felt the man pulling away from her. He's very strong, she thought. 'How come you're so strong?' she asked, gasping for air; she found herself almost unable to breathe.

'Carry rocks,' he said with a grin.

I want him, she thought. Big, evil, powerful . . . he could tear me to pieces, she thought. Her longing for him grew.

'I'll get you,' she gasped, 'because I want you.' I need to have you, she said to herself. Covering me like a heavy shade, a protection from the sun and from seeing. I don't want to look any more, she said to herself. Weigh me down, she thought. Show me what there is of you; show me your real being, without benefit of clothes. Fumbling behind her she unsnapped her peek-n-squeeze bra. Deftly she tugged it out from its place within her sweater; she pulled, strained, managed to drop it on to a chair. At that the man laughed. 'Why are you laughing?' she demanded.

'Your neatness,' he said. 'Getting it on to a chair instead of dropping it on to the floor.'

'Damn you,' she said, knowing that he, like everyone else, was laughing at her. 'I'll get you,' she snarled, and pulled him with all her strength; this time she managed to move him a few tottering steps in the direction of the bed.

'Hey, goddam it,' he protested. But again she managed to move him several steps. 'Stop!' he said. And then she had tumbled him on to the bed. She held him down with one knee and rapidly, with great expertise, unsnapped her skirt and pushed it from the bed, on to the floor.

'See?' she said. 'I don't have to be neat.' She dived for him then; she pinned him down with her knees. 'I'm not obsessive,' she said, as she removed the last of her clothing. Now she tore at the buttons of his shirt. A button, ripped loose, rolled like a little wheel from the bed and on to the floor. At that she laughed. She felt very good. This part always excited her – it was like the final stage of a hunt, in this case a hunt for a big animal which smelled of sweat and of cigarette smoke and of agitated fear. How can he be afraid of me? she asked herself, but it was always this way – she had come to accept it. In fact she had come to like it.

'Let – me – go,' he gasped, pushing upward against her weight. 'You're so darn – slippery,' he managed to say as she gripped his head with her knees.

'I can make you so happy, sexually,' she told him; she always said this, and sometimes it worked; sometimes the man gave in at the prospect she held open to him. 'Come on,' she said, in rapid, imploring grunts.

The door of the room banged open. Immediately, instinctively, she sprang from the man, from the bed, stood upright, breathing noisily, peering at the figure in the doorway. His wife. Mary Morley. Susie at once snatched up her clothes; this was one part which she did not enjoy, and she felt overwhelming hatred toward Mary Morley. 'Get out of here,' Susie panted. 'This is my room.'

'Seth!' Mary Morley said in a shrill voice. 'What in the name of God is the matter with you? *How could you do this?*' She moved stiffly toward the bed, her face pale.

'God,' Morley said, sitting up and smoothing his hair into place. 'This girl is nuts,' he said to his wife in a plaintive, whining tone. 'I had nothing to do with it; I was trying to get away. You saw that, didn't you? Couldn't you tell I was trying to get away? Didn't you see that?'

Mary Morley said in her shrill, speeded-up voice, 'If you had wanted to get away you could have.'

'No,' he said imploringly. 'Really, so help me God. She had me pinned down. I was getting loose, though. If you hadn't come in I would have gotten away by myself.'

'I'll kill you,' Mary Morley said; she spun, paced about in a great circle which swept out most of the room. Looking for something to pick up and hit with; Susie knew the motion, the searching, the glazed, ferocious, incredulous expression on her face. Mary Morley found a vase, snatched it up, stood by the dresser, her chest heaving as she confronted Seth Morley. She raised the vase in a spasmodic, abrupt, backward swing of her right arm ...

On the dresser the miniaturized building slid a minute panel aside. A tiny cannon projected. Mary did not see it, but Susie and Seth Morley did.

'Look out!' Seth gasped, groping at his wife to get hold of her hand. He yanked her towards him. The vase crashed to the floor. The barrel of the cannon rotated, taking new aim. All at once a beam projected from it, in Mary Morley's direction. Susie laughed, backed away, putting distance between herself and the beam.

The beam missed Mary Morley. On the far wall of the room a hole appeared and through it black night air billowed, cold and harsh, entering the room. Mary wobbled, retreated a step.

Rushing into the bathroom, Seth Morley disappeared, then came dashing out again, the water glass in his hand.

He sprinted to the dresser, poured water on to the building replica. The snout of the cannon ceased to rotate.

'I think I got it,' Seth Morley said, wheezing asthmatically.

From the diminutive structure a curl of grey smoke drifted up. The structure hummed briefly and then a pool of sticky, grease-like stain dribbled out from it, mixing with the pool of water which had now formed around it. The structure bucked, spun, and then all at once decayed into inanimation. He was right; it was dead.

'You killed it,' Susie said, accusingly.

Seth Morley said, 'That's what killed Tallchief.'

'Did it try to kill me?' Mary Morley asked faintly. She looked about unsteadily, the fanaticism of fury gone from her face now. Cautiously, she seated herself and stared at the structure, blank and pale, then said to her husband, 'Let's get out of here.'

To Susie, Seth Morley said, 'I'm going to have to tell Glen Belsnor.' He gingerly, and with great caution, picked up the little dead block; holding it in the palm of his hand he stared at it a long, long time.

'It took me three weeks to tame that one,' Susie said. 'Now I have to find another, and bring it back here without getting killed, and tame it like I did this one.' She felt massive waves of accusation slapping higher and higher within her. 'Look what you did,' she said, and went swiftly to gather up her clothing.

Seth and Mary Morley started towards the door, Seth's hand on his wife's back. Guiding her out.

'Goddam you both!' she shouted in accusation. Half-dressed, she followed after them. 'What about tomorrow?' she said to Seth. 'Are we still going on a walk? I want to show you some of the—'

'No,' he said harshly, and then he turned to gaze at her long and sombrely. 'You really don't understand what happened,' he said.

Susie said, 'I know what *almost* happened.'

'Does someone have to die before you can wake up?' he said.

'No,' she said, feeling uneasy; she did not like the expression in his hard, boring eyes. 'All right,' she said, 'if it's so important to you, that little toy—'

'"Toy",' he said mockingly.

'Toy,' she repeated. 'Then you ought to be really interested in what's out there. Don't you understand? This is just a model of the real Building. Don't you want to see it? I've seen it very closely. I even know what the sign reads over the main entrance. Not the entrance where the trucks come and go but the entrance—'

'What does it say?' he said.

Susie said, 'Will you go with me?' To Mary Morley she said, with all the graciousness she could command, 'You, too. Both of you ought to come.'

'I'll come alone,' Seth said. To his wife he said, 'It's too dangerous; I don't want you along.'

'You don't want me along,' Mary said, 'for obvious other reasons.' But she sounded dim and scared, as if the close call with the structure's energy beam had banished every emotion in her except raw, clinging fear.

Seth Morley said, 'What does it say over the entrance?'

After a pause Susie said, 'It says "Whippery".'

'What does that mean?' he said.

'I'm not positive. But it sounds fascinating. Maybe we can somehow get inside, this time. I've gone real close, almost up to the wall. But I couldn't find a side door, and I was afraid – I don't know why – to go in the main entrance.'

Wordlessly, Seth Morley, steering his dazed wife, strode out into the night. She found herself standing there in the middle of her room, alone and only half-dressed.

'Bitch!' she called loudly after them. Meaning Mary.

They continued on. And were gone from sight.

SEVEN

'Don't kid yourself,' Glen Belsnor said. 'If it shot at your wife it's because that loopy dame, that Susie Dumb or Smart, whichever it is, wanted it to. She taught it. They can be trained, you see.' He sat holding the tiny structure, staring down at it, a brooding expression settling by degrees in to his long, lean face.

'If I hadn't grabbed her,' Seth said, 'we would have had a second death tonight.'

'Maybe yes, maybe no. Considering the meagre output of these things it probably would only have knocked her out.'

'The beam bored through the wall.'

Belsnor said, 'The walls are cheap plastic. One layer. You could punch a hole through with your fist.'

'So you're not upset by this.'

Belsnor plucked at his lower lip thoughtfully. 'I'm upset by the whole thing. What the hell were you doing with Susie in her room?' He raised his hand. 'Don't tell me, I know. She's deranged sexually. No, don't give me any details.' He played aimlessly with the replica of the Building. 'Too bad it didn't shoot Susie,' he murmured, half to himself.

'There's something the matter with all of you,' Seth said.

Belsnor raised his shaggy head and studied Seth Morley. 'In what way?'

'I'm not sure. A kind of idiocy. Each of you seems to be living in his own private world. Without regard for any-one else. It's as if—' He pondered. 'As if all you want, each of you, is to be left alone.'

'No,' Belsnor said. 'We want to get away from here. We

may have nothing else in common, but we do share that.'
He handed the destroyed structure back to Seth. 'Keep it.
As a souvenir.'

Seth tossed it on to the floor.

'You're going out exploring with Susie tomorrow?' Belsnor said.

'Yes.' He nodded.

'She'll probably attack you again.'

'I'm not interested in that. I'm not worried by that. I think that we have an active enemy on the planet, working from outside the settlement area. I think it – or they – killed Tallchief. Despite what Babble found.'

Belsnor said, 'You're new here. Tallchief was new here. Tallchief is dead. I think there's a connection; I think his death was connected to his unfamiliarity with the conditions on this planet. Therefore you're equally in danger. But the rest of us—'

'You don't think I should go.'

'Go, yes. But be very careful. Don't touch anything, don't pick up anything, keep your eyes open. Try to go only where she's been; don't tackle new areas.'

'Why don't you come too?'

Regarding him intently, Belsnor said, 'You want me to?'

'You're the settlement's leader, now. Yes, I think you should come. And armed.'

'I—' Belsnor pondered. 'It could be argued that I ought to stay here and work on the transmitter. It could be argued that you ought to be at work composing a prayer, instead of tramping around in the wilderness. I have to think of every aspect of this situation. It could be argued—'

'It could be argued that your "could be argueds" may kill us all,' Seth Morley said.

'Your "could be argued" may be correct.' Belsnor smiled as if at a private, secret reality. The smile, with no amusement in it, lingered on his face; it remained and became sardonic.

77

Seth Morley said, 'Tell me what you know about the ecology out there.'

'There is an organism which we call the tench. There are, we've gathered, five or six of them. Very old.'

'What do they do? Are they artifact makers?'

'Some, the feeble ones, do nothing. They just sit there, here and there in the middle of the landscape. The less feeble ones, however, print.'

'Print?'

'They duplicate things brought to them. Small things, such as a wristwatch, a cup, an electric razor.'

'And the printings work?'

Belsnor tapped his jacket pocket. 'The pen I'm using is a print. But—' He lifted out the pen and extended it towards Seth Morley. 'See the decay?' The surface of the pen had a furry texture, much like dust. 'They decompose very rapidly. This'll be good for another few days, and then I can have another print made from the original pen.'

'Why?'

'Because we're short of pens. And the ones we have are running out of ink.'

'What about the writing of one of these print-pens? Does the ink fade out after a few days?'

'No,' Belsnor said, but he looked uncomfortable.

'You're not sure.'

Standing, Belsnor dug into his back pocket and got out his wallet. For a time he examined small, folded pieces of paper and then placed one in front of Seth. The writing was clear and distinct.

Maggie Walsh entered the briefing chamber, saw the two of them, and came over. 'May I join you?'

'Sure,' Belsnor said remotely. 'Pull up a chair.' He glanced at Seth Morley, then said to her in a leisurely, hard voice, 'Susie Smart's toy building tried to shoot Morley's wife a while ago. It missed, and Morley poured a plate of water over it.'

78

'I warned her,' Maggie said, 'that those things are unsafe.'

'It was safe enough,' Belsnor said. 'It's Susie that isn't safe . . . as I was explaining to Morley.'

'We should pray for her,' Maggie said.

'You see?' Belsnor said to Seth Morley. 'We do have concern for one another. Maggie wants to save Susie Smart's immortal soul.'

'Pray,' Seth Morley said, 'that she doesn't capture another replica and begin teaching that one, too.'

'Morley,' Belsnor said, 'I've been thinking about your thoughts on the whole bunch of us. In a way you're right: there is something the matter with each of us. But not what you think. The thing we have in common is that we're failures. Take Tallchief. Couldn't you tell he's a wino? And Susie – all she can think about is sexual conquests. I can make a guess about you, too. You're overweight; obviously you eat too much. Do you live to eat, Morley? Or had you never asked yourself that? Babble is a hypochondriac. Betty Jo Berm is a compulsive pilltaker: her life is in those little plastic bottles. That kid, Tony Dunkelwelt; he lives for his mystical insights, his schizophrenic trances . . . which both Babble and Frazer call catatonic stupor. Maggie, here—' He gestured toward her. 'She lives in an illusory world of prayer and fasting, doing service to a deity which isn't interested in her.' To Maggie he said, 'Have you ever seen the Intercessor, Maggie?'

She shook her head no.

'Or the Walker-on-Earth?'

'No,' she said.

'Nor the Mentufacturer either,' Belsnor said. 'Now take Wade Frazer. His world—'

'How about you?' Seth asked him.

Belsnor shrugged. 'I have my own world.'

'He invents,' Maggie Walsh said.

79

'But I've never invented anything,' Belsnor said. 'Everything developed during the last two centuries has come from a composite lab, where hundreds, even thousands of research workers work. There is no such thing as an inventor in this century. Maybe I just like to play private games with electronic components. Anyhow, I enjoy it. I get most if not all of my pleasure in this world from creating circuits that ultimately do nothing.'

'A dream of fame,' Maggie said.

'No.' Belsnor shook his head. 'I want to contribute something; I don't want to be just a consumer, like the rest of you.' His tone was hard and flat and very earnest. 'We live in a world created and manufactured from the results of the work of millions of men, most of them dead, virtually none of them given any credit. I don't care if I'm known for what I create; all I care about is having it be worthwhile and useful, with people able to depend on it as something they take for granted in their lives. Like the safety pin. Who knows who created that? But everyone in the goddam galaxy makes use of safety pins, and the inventor—'

'Safety pins were invented on Crete,' Seth Morley said. 'In the fourth or fifth century BC.'

Belsnor glared at him. 'About one thousand BC.'

'So it matters to you when and where they were invented,' Seth Morley said.

'I came close to producing something one time,' Belsnor said. 'A silencing circuit. It would have interrupted the flow of electrons in any given conductor for a range of about fifty feet. As a weapon of defence it would have been valuable. But I couldn't get the field to propagate for fifty feet; I could only get it functional for one-and-a-half feet. So that was that.' He lapsed into silence, then. Brooding, baleful silence. Withdrawn into himself.

'We love you anyway,' Maggie said.

Belsnor raised his head and glared at her.

'The Deity accepts even that,' Maggie said. 'Even an attempt which led nowhere. The Deity knows your motive, and motive is everything.'

'It wouldn't matter,' Belsnor said, 'if this whole colony, everybody in it, died. None of us contribute anything. We're nothing more than parasites, feeding off the galaxy. "The world will little note nor long remember what we do here".'

Seth Morley said to Maggie. 'Our leader. The man who's going to keep us alive.'

'I'll keep you alive,' Belsnor said. 'As best I can. That could be my contribution: inventing a device made out of fluid-state circuitry that'll save us. That'll spike all the toy cannons.'

'I don't think you're very bright to call something a toy simply because its small,' Maggie Walsh said. 'That would mean that the Toxilax artificial kidney is a toy.'

'You would have to call eighty per cent of all Interplan ship circuitry toys,' Seth Morley said.

'Maybe that's my problem,' Belsnor said wryly 'I can't tell what's a toy and what isn't . . . which means I can't tell what's real. A toy ship is not a real ship. A toy cannon is not a real cannon. But I guess if it can kill—' He pondered. 'Perhaps tomorrow I should require everyone to go systematically through the settlement, collecting all the toy buildings, in fact everything from outside, and then we'll ignite the whole pile and be done with it.'

'What else has come into the settlement from outside?' Seth Morley inquired.

'Artificial flies,' Belsnor said. 'For one thing.'

'They take pictures?' Seth asked.

'No, that's the artificial bees. The artificial flies fly around and sing.'

' "Sing"?' He thought he must have heard wrong.

'I have one here.' Belsnor rummaged in his pockets and at last brought out a small plastic box. 'Hold it to your ear. There's one in there.'

'What sort of thing do they sing?' Seth Morley held the

box to his ear, listened. He heard it, then, a far-off sweet sound, like divided strings. And, he thought, like many distant wings. 'I know that music,' he said, 'but I can't place it.' An indistinct favourite of mine, he realized. From some ancient era.

'They play what you like,' Maggie Walsh said.

He recognized it now. 'Granada.' 'I'll be goddamed,' he said aloud. 'Are you sure it's a fly that's doing that?'

'Look in the box,' Belsnor said. 'But be careful – don't let it out. They're rare and hard to catch.'

With great care Seth Morley slid back the lid of the box. He saw within it a dark fly, like a Proxima 6 tape-fly, large and hairy, with beating wings and eyes protruding, composite eyes, such as true flies had. He shut the box, convinced. 'Amazing,' he said. 'Is it acting as a receiver? Picking up a signal from a central transmitter somewhere on the planet? 'It's a radio – is that it?'

'I took one apart,' Belsnor said. 'It's not a receiver; the music is emitted by a speaker but it emanates from the fly's works. The signal is created by a miniature generator in the form of an electrical impulse, not unlike a nerve impulse in an organic living creature. There's a moist element ahead of the generator which alters a complex pattern of conductivity, so a very complex signal can be created. What's it singing for you?'

' "Granada",' Seth Morley said. He wished he could keep it. The fly would be company for him. 'Will you sell it?' he asked.

'Catch your own.' Belsnor retrieved his fly and placed the box back in his pocket.

'Is there anything else from outside the settlement?' Seth Morley asked. 'Besides the bees, flies, printers and miniature buildings?'

Maggie Walsh said, 'A sort of flea-sized printer. But it can only print one thing; it does it over and over again, grinding out a flood that seems endless.'

'A print of what?'

82

'Of Specktowsky's Book,' Maggie Walsh said.

'And that's it?'

'That's all we know about,' Maggie amended. 'There may be others unknown to us.' She shot a sharp glance at Belsnor.

Belsnor said nothing; he had again retracted into his own personal world, for the moment, oblivious to them.

Seth Morley picked up the abolished miniature building and said, 'If the tenches only print duplicates of objects then they didn't make this. Something with highly-developed technical skills would have had to.'

'It could have been made centuries ago,' Belsnor said, rousing himself. 'By a race that's no longer here.'

'And printed continually since?'

'Yes. Or printed after we arrived here. For our benefit.'

'How long do these miniature buildings last? Longer than your pen?'

'I see what you mean,' Belsnor said. 'No, they don't seem to decay rapidly. Maybe they're not printings. I don't see that it makes much difference; they could have been held in reserve all this time. Put aside until needed, until something along the lines of our colony manifested itself.'

'Is there a microscope here in the settlement?'

'Sure.' Belsnor nodded. 'Babble has one.'

'I'll go see Babble, then.' Seth Morley moved toward the door of the briefing chamber. 'Goodnight,' he said, over his shoulder.

Neither of them answered; they seemed indifferent to him and to what he had said. Will I be this way in a couple of weeks? he asked himself. It was a good question, and before long he would have the answer.

'Yes,' Babble said. 'You can use my microscope.' He had on pyjamas and slippers and an ersatz-wool striped bathrobe. 'I was just going to bed.' He watched Seth Morley bring forth the miniature building. 'Oh, one of those. They're all over the place.'

Seating himself at the microscope, Seth Morley pried open the tiny structure, broke away the outer hull, then placed the component-complex on to the stage of the microscope. He used the low-power resolution, obtaining a magnification of 600x.

Intricate strands ... printed circuitry, of course, on a series of modules. Resistors, condensers, valves. A power supply: one ultra-miniaturized helium battery. He could make out the swivel of the cannon barrel and what appeared to be the germanium arc which served as the source of the energy beam. It can't be very strong, he realized. Belsnor in a sense was right: the output, in ergs, must be terribly small.

He focused on the motor which drove the cannon barrel as it moved from side to side. Words were printed on the hasp which held the barrel in place; he strained to read them – and saw, as he adjusted the fine focus of the microscope, a confirmation of what he most feared.

MADE AT TERRA 35082R

The construct had come from Earth. It had not been invented by a superterrestial race – it did not emanate from the native life forms of Delmak-O. So much for that.

General Treaton, he said to himself grimly. It is you, after all, who is destroying us. Our transmitter, our receiver – and the demand that we reach this planet by noser. Was it you who had Ben Tallchief killed? Obviously.

'What are you finding there?' Babble asked.

'I am finding,' he said, 'that General Treaton is our enemy and that we don't have a chance.' He moved away from the microscope. 'Take a look.'

Babble placed his eye against the eye-piece of the microscope. 'Nobody thought of that,' he said presently. 'We could have examined one of these any time during the last

84

two months. It just never occurred to us.' He looked away from the microscope, peering falteringly at Seth Morley. 'What'll we do?'

'The first thing is to collect all of these, everything brought into the settlement from outside, and destroy them.'

'That means the Building is Earth-made.'

'Yes.' Seth Morley nodded. Evidently so, he thought. 'We are part of an experiment,' he said.

'We've got to get off this planet,' Babble said.

'We'll never get off,' Seth Morley said.

'It must all be coming from the Building. We've got to find a way to destroy it. But I don't see how we can.'

'Do you want to revise your autopsy report on Tall-chief?'

'I have nothing more to go on. At this point I'd say he was probably killed by a weapon that we know nothing about. Something that generates fatal amounts of histamine in the blood supply. Which brings on what looks like a natural breathing-apparatus involvement. There is another possibility which you might consider. It could be a forgery. After all, Earth has become one giant mental hospital.'

'There are military research labs there. Highly secret ones. The general public doesn't know about them.'

'How do you know about them?'

Seth Morley said, 'At Tekel Upharsin, as the kibbutz's marine biologist, I had dealings with them. And when we bought weapons.' Strictly speaking, this was not true; he had, really, only heard rumours. But the rumours had convinced him.

'Tell me,' Babble said, eyeing him, 'did you really see the Walker-on-Earth?'

'Yes,' he said. 'And I know first hand about the secret military research labs on Terra. For example—'

Babble said, 'You saw someone. I believe that. Someone whom you didn't know came up and pointed out something that should have been obvious to you: namely, that the noser you had picked out was not spaceworthy. But you had it already in your mind – because it was taught to you throughout childhood – that if a stranger came to you and offered unsolicited help, that that stranger had to be a Manifestation of the Deity. But look: what you saw was what you expected to see. You assumed that he was the Walker-on-Earth because Specktowsky's Book is virtually universally accepted. But I don't accept it.'

'You don't?' Seth Morley said, surprised.

'Not at all. Strangers – true strangers, ordinary men – show up and give good advice; most humans are well-intentioned. If I had happened by I would have intervened too. I would have pointed out that your ship wasn't spaceworthy.'

'Then you would have been in the possession of the Walker-on-Earth; you would have temporarily become him. It can happen to anyone. That's part of the miracle.'

'There are no miracles. As Spinoza proved centuries ago. A miracle would be a sign of God's weakness, as a failure of natural law. If there were a God.'

Seth Morley said, 'You told us, earlier this evening, that you saw the Walker-on-Earth seven times.' Suspicion filled him; he had caught the inconsistency. 'And the Intercessor too.'

'What I meant by that,' Babble said smoothly, 'is that I encountered life-situations in which human beings *acted* as the Walker-on-Earth would have acted, did he exist. Your problem is that of a lot of people: it stems from our having encountered non-humanoid sentient races, some of them, the ones we call "gods", on what we call "god-worlds", so much superior to us as to put us in – for example – the role that, say, dogs or cats have to us. To a dog or a cat a man seems like God: he can do god-like things. But the quasi-biological, ultra-sentient life forms on god-worlds – they're just as much the products of natural biological evolution as we are. In time we may

86

evolve that far ... even farther. I'm not saying we will, I'm saying we can.' He pointed his finger determinedly at Seth Morley. 'They didn't create the universe. They're not Manifestations of the Mentufacturer. All we have is their verbal report that they are Manifestations of the Deity. Why should we believe them? Naturally, if we ask them, "Are you God? Did you make the universe?" they'll reply in the affirmative. We'd do the same thing; white men, back in the sixteenth and seventeenth centuries, told the natives of North and South America exactly the same thing'.

'But the Spanish and English and French were colonists. They had a motive for pretending to be gods. Take Cortez. He—'

'The life forms on so-called "god-worlds" have a similar motive.'

'Like what?' He felt his dull anger beginning to glow. 'They're saint-like. They contemplate; they listen to our prayers – if they can pick them up – and they act to fulfil our prayers. As they did, for example, with Ben Tallchief.'

'They sent him here to die. Is that right?'

That had been acutely bothering him, starting at the moment he had first caught sight of Tallchief's dead and inert body. 'Maybe they didn't know,' he said uncomfortably. 'After all, Specktowsky points out that the Deity does not know everything. For instance. He did not know that the Form Destroyer existed, or that He'd be awakened by the concentric rings of emanation that make up the universe. Or that the Form Destroyer would enter the universe, and hence time, and corrupt the universe that the Mentufacturer had made in his own image, so that it was no longer his image.'

'Just like Maggie Walsh. She talks the same way.' Dr Babble barked out a harsh, short laugh.

Seth Morley said, 'I've never met an atheist before.' In actuality he had met one, but it had been years ago. 'It seems very strange in this era, when we have proof of the Deity's existence. I can understand there being widespread atheism in previous eras, when religion was based on faith in things unseen . . . but now it's not unseen, as Specktowsky indicated.'

'The Walker-on-Earth,' Babble said sardonically, 'is a sort of anti-Person-from-Porlock. Instead of interfering with a good process or event he—' Babble broke off.

The door of the infirmary had opened. A man stood there, wearing a soft plastic work-jacket, semi-leather pants and boots. He was dark-haired, probably in his late thirties, with a strong face; his cheekbones were high and his eyes were large and bright. He carried a flashlight, which he now shut off. He stood there, gazing at Babble and Seth Morley, saying nothing. Merely standing silent and waiting. Seth Morley thought, *This is a resident of the settlement that I've never seen.* And then, noticing Babble's expression, *he realized that Babble had never seen him either.*

'Who are you?' Babble said hoarsely.

The man said in a low, mild voice, 'I just arrived here in my noser. My name is Ned Russell. I'm an economist.' He held out his hand toward Babble, who accepted it reflexively.

'I thought everyone was here,' Babble said. 'We have thirteen people; that's all there's supposed to be.'

'I applied for a transfer and this was the destination. Delmak-O.' Russell turned to Seth Morley, again holding out his hand. The two men shook.

'Let's see your transfer order,' Babble said.

Russell dug into his coat pocket. 'This is a strange place you're operating here. Almost no lights, the automatic pilot inoperative . . . I had to land it myself and I'm not that used to a noser. I parked it with all the others, in the field at the edge of your settlement.'

'So we have two points to raise with Belsnor,' Seth Morley said. 'The made-at-Terra inscription on the miniaturized building. And him.' He wondered which would prove to be the more important. At the moment he could not see clearly enough ahead to know one way or the other. Something to save us, he thought; something to doom us. It – the equation of everything – could go either way.

In the nocturnal darkness Susie Smart slipped by degrees in the direction of Tony Dunkelwelt's living quarters. She wore a black slip and high heels – knowing that the boy liked that.

Knock, knock.

'Who is it?' a voice mumbled from within.

'Susie.' She tried the knob. The door was unlocked. So she went ahead on in.

In the centre of the room Tony Dunkelwelt sat cross-legged on the floor in front of a single candle. His eyes, in the dim light, were shut; evidently he was in a trance. He showed no signs of noticing her or recognizing her, and yet he had asked her name. 'Is it all right for me to come in?'

His trance-states worried her. In them he withdrew entirely from the regular world. Sometimes he sat this way for hours, and when they questioned the boy about what he saw he could give little or no answer.

'I don't mean to butt in,' she said, when he did not answer.

In a modulated, detached voice, Tony said, 'Welcome.'

'Thank you,' she said, relieved. Seating herself in a straight-backed chair she found her package of cigarettes, lit one, settled back for what she knew would be a long wait. But she did not feel like waiting.

Cautiously, she kick-kicked at him with the toe of her high heeled shoe. 'Tony?' she said. 'Tony?'

'Yes,' he said.

'Tell me, Tony, what do you see? Another world? Can you see all the busy gods running about doing good deeds? Can you see the Form Destroyer at work? How does he look?' No one ever saw the Form Destroyer except Tony

Dunkelwelt. He had the principle of evil all to himself. And it was this frightening quality about the boy's trances which kept her from trying to interfere; when he was in a trance-state she tried to leave him alone, to work his way back from his vision of pure malignancy to their normal and everyday responsibility.

'Don't talk to me,' Tony mumbled. He had his eyes squeezed shut, and his face was pinched and red.

'Knock off for a while,' she said. 'You ought to be in bed. Do you want to go to bed, Tony? With me, for example?' She placed her hand on his shoulder; by degrees he then slid away, until she was holding nothing. 'You remember what you said about me loving you because you're not yet a real man? You are a real man. Wouldn't I know? Leave the deciding up to me: I'll tell you when you're a man and when you're not, if you ever happen to be not. But up until now you've been more than a man. Did you know that an eighteen-year-old can have seven orgasms in one twenty-four-hour period?' She waited, but he said nothing. 'That's pretty good,' she said.

Tony said raptly, 'There is a deity above the Deity. One who embraces all four.'

'What four? Four what?'

'The four Manifestations. The Mentufacturer, the—'

'Who's the fourth?'

'The Form Destroyer.'

'You mean that you can commune with a god that combines the Form Destroyer with the other three? But that's not possible, Tony; they are good gods and the Form Destroyer is evil.'

'I know that,' he said in a sullen voice. 'That's why what I see is so keen. A god-above-god, which no one can see but me.' Again, by degrees, he drifted back into his trance; he ceased speaking to her.

'How come you can see something that no one else can, and still call it real?' Susie asked. 'Specktowsky didn't say anything about such a super Deity. I think it's all in your own mind.' She felt cross and cold, and the cigarette burned her nose; she had, as usual, been smoking too much. 'Let's go to bed, Tony,' she said vigorously, and stubbed out her cigarette. 'Come on.' Bending, she took hold of him by the arm. But he remained inert. Like a rock.

Time passed. He communed on and on.

'Jesus!' she said angrily. 'Well the hell with it; I'll leave. Goodnight.' Rising, she walked rapidly to the door, opened it, stood half inside and half out. 'We could have so much fun if we went to bed,' she said plaintively. 'Is there something about me you don't like? I mean, I could change it. And I've been reading; there're several positions I didn't know. Let me teach them to you; they sound like a lot of fun.'

Tony Dunkelwelt opened his eyes and, unwinkingly, regarded her. She could not decipher the expression on his face, and it made her uneasy; she began rubbing her bare arms and shivering.

'The Form Destroyer,' Tony said, 'is absolutely-not-God.'

'I realize that,' she said.

'But "absolutely-not-God" is a category of being.'

'If you say so, Tony.'

'And God contains all categories of being. Therefore God can be absolutely-not-God, which transcends human reason and logic. But we intuitively feel it to be so. Don't you? Wouldn't you prefer a monism that transcends our pitiful dualism? Specktowsky was a great man, but there is a higher monistic structure above the dualism that he foresaw. *There is a higher God.*' He eyed her. 'What do you think about that?' he asked, a little timidly.

'I think it's wonderful,' Susie said, with enthusiasm. 'It must be so great to have trances and perceive what you perceive. You should write a book saying that what Specktowsky says is wrong.'

'It's not wrong,' Tony said. 'It's transcended by what I

see. When you get to that level, two opposite things can be equal. That's what I'm trying to reveal.'

'Couldn't you reveal it tomorrow?' she asked, still shivering and massaging her bare arms. 'I'm so cold and so tired and I had an awful run-in with that goddam Mary Morley tonight already, so come on, please; let's go to bed.'

'I'm a prophet,' Tony said. 'Like Christ or Moses or Specktowsky. I will never be forgotten.' Again he shut his eyes. The weak candle flickered and almost went out. He did not notice.

'If you're a prophet,' Susie said, 'perform a miracle.' She had read in Specktowsky's Book about that, about the prophets having miraculous powers. 'Prove it to me,' she said.

One eye opened. 'Why must you have a sign?'

'I don't want a sign. I want a miracle.'

'A miracle,' he said, 'is a sign. All right, I'll do something that will show you.' He gazed around the room, his face holding a deeply-ingrained resentment. She had awakened him now, she realized. And he didn't like it.

'Your face is turning black,' she said.

He touched his brow experimentally. 'It's turning red. But the candle light doesn't contain a full light spectrum so it looks black.' He slid to his feet and walked stiffly about, rubbing the base of his neck.

'How long were you sitting there?' she asked.

'I don't know.'

'That's right; you lose all conception of time.' She had heard him say it. That part alone awed her. 'Okay,' she said, 'turn this into a stone.' She had found a loaf of bread, a jar of peanut butter, and a knife; holding up the loaf of bread she moved towards him, feeling mischievous. 'Can you do that?'

Solemnly, he said, 'The opposite of Christ's miracle.'

'Can you do it?'

He accepted the loaf of bread from her, held it with

both hands; he gazed down at it, his lips moving. His entire face began to writhe, as if with tremendous effort. The darkness grew; his eyes faded out and were replaced by impenetrable buttons of darkness.

The loaf of bread flipped from his hands, rose until it hung well above him . . . it twisted, became hazy, and then, like a stone, it dropped to the floor. *Like* a stone? She knelt down to stare at it, wondering if the light of the room had put her into a hypnotic trance. The loaf of bread was gone. What rested on the floor appeared to be a smooth, large rock, a water-tumbled rock, with pale sides. 'My good God,' she said, half aloud. 'Can I pick it up? Is it safe?'

Tony, his eyes once more filled with life, also knelt and stared at it. 'God's power,' he said, 'was in me. I didn't do that; it was done *through* me.'

Picking up the rock – it was heavy – she discovered that it felt warm and nearly alive. An animate rock, she said to herself. As if it's organic. Maybe it's not a real rock. She banged it against the floor; it felt hard enough, and it made the right noise. It is a rock, she realized. It is!

'Can I have it?' she asked. Her awe had become complete now; she gazed at him hopefully, willing to do exactly what he said.

'You may have it, Suzanne,' Tony said in a calm voice. 'But arise and go back to your room. I'm tired.' He did sound tired, and his entire body drooped. 'I'll see you in the morning at breakfast. Goodnight.'

'Goodnight,' she said, 'but I can undress you and put you to bed; I'd enjoy that.'

'No,' he said. He went to the door and held it open for her.

'Kiss.' Coming up to him she leaned forward and kissed him on the lips. 'Thank you,' she said, feeling humble. 'Goodnight, Tony. And thanks for the miracle.' The door started to close behind her but, adroitly, she stopped it with the wedge-shaped toe of her shoe. 'Can I tell everyone about this? I mean, isn't this the first miracle you've ever

93

done? Shouldn't they know? But if you don't want them to know I won't tell them.'

'Let me sleep,' he said, and shut the door; it clicked in her face and she felt animal terror – this was what she feared most in life: the clicking shut of a man's door in her face. Instantly, she raised her hand to knock, discovered the rock ... she banged on the door with the rock, but not loudly, just enough to let him know how desperate she was to get back in, but not loudly enough to bother him if he didn't want to answer.

He didn't. No sound, no movement of the door. Nothing but the void.

'Tony?' she gasped, pressing her ear to the door. Silence. 'Okay,' she said numbly; clutching her rock she walked unsteadily across the porch towards her own living quarters.

The rock vanished. Her hand felt nothing.

'Damn,' she said, not knowing how to react. Where had it gone? Into air. But then it must have been an illusion, she realized. He put me in a hypnotic state and made me believe. I should have known it wasn't really true.

A million stars burst into wheels of light, blistering, cold light, that drenched her. It came from behind and she felt the great weight of it crash into her. 'Tony,' she said, and fell into the waiting void. She thought nothing; she felt nothing. She saw only, saw the void as it absorbed her, waiting below and beneath her as she plummeted down the many miles.

On her hands and knees she died. Alone on the porch. Still clutching for what did not exist.

EIGHT

Glen Belsnor lay dreaming. In the dark of night he dreamed of himself; he perceived himself as he really was, a wise and beneficial provider. Happily he thought, I can do it. I can take care of them all, help them and protect them. They must be protected at all costs, he thought to himself in his dream.

In his dream he attached connecting cable, screwed a circuit-breaker in place, tried out a servo-assist unit.

A hum rose from the elaborate mechanism. A generated field, miles high, rose in every direction. No one can get past that, he said to himself in satisfaction, and some of his fear began to dwindle away. The colony is safe and I have done it.

In the colony the people moved back and forth, wearing long red robes. It became midday and then it became midday for a thousand years. He saw, all at once, that they had become old. Tottering, with tattered beards – the women, too – they crept about in a feeble, insect-like manner. And some of them, he saw, were blind.

Then we're not safe, he realized. Even with the field in operation. They were fading away from inside. They will all die anyhow.

'Belsnor!'

He opened his eyes and knew what it was.

Grey, early-morning sunlight filtered through the shades of his room. Seven AM, he saw by his self-winding wristwatch. He rose up to a sitting position, pushing the covers away. Chill morning air plucked at him and he shivered. 'Who?' he said to the men and women pouring into his room. He shut his eyes, grimaced, felt, despite the emergency, the rancid remains of sleep still clinging to him.

Ignatz Thugg, wearing gaily decorated pyjamas, said loudly, 'Susie Smart.'

Putting on his bathrobe, Belsnor moved numbly towards the door.

'Do you know what this means?' Wade Frazer said.

'Yes,' he said. 'I know exactly what it means.'

Roberta Rockingham, touching the corner of a small linen handkerchief to her eyes, said, 'She was such a bright spirit, always lighting up things with her presence. How could anybody do it to her?' A trail of tears materialized on her withered cheeks.

He made his way across the compound; the others clumped after him, none of them speaking.

There she lay, on the porch. A few steps from her door. He bent over her, touched the back of her neck. Absolutely cold. No life of any kind. 'You examined her?' he said to Babble. 'She really is dead? There's no doubt about it?'

'Look at your hand,' Wade Frazer said.

Belsnor removed his hand from the girl's neck. His hand dripped blood. And now he saw the mass of blood in her hair, near the top of her skull. Her head had been crushed in.

'Care to revise your autopsy?' he said scathingly to Babble. 'Your opinion about Tallchief; do you care to change it now?'

No one spoke.

Belsnor looked around, saw not far off a loaf of bread. 'She must have been carrying that,' he said.

'She got it from me,' Tony Dunkelwelt said. His face had paled from shock; his words were barely audible. 'She left my room last night and I went to bed. I didn't kill her. I didn't even know about it until I heard Dr Babble and the others yelling.'

'We're not saying you did it,' Belsnor said to him. Yes, she used to flit from one room to another at night, he thought. We made fun of her and she was a little deranged

. . . but she never hurt anybody. She was as innocent as a human being could get; she was even innocent of her own wrong-doing.

The new man, Russell, approached. The expression on his face showed that he, too, without even knowing her, understood what an awful thing it was, what an awful moment it was for all of them.

'You see what you came here to see?' Belsnor said to him harshly.

Russell said, 'I wonder if you could get help by means of the transmitter in my noser.'

'They're not good enough,' Belsnor said. 'The noser radio-rig. Not good enough at all.' He rose to his feet stiffly, hearing his bones crack. And it's Terra that's doing this, he thought, remembering what Seth Morley and Babble had said last night when they brought Russell over. Our own government. As if we're rats in a maze with death; rodents confined with the ultimate adversary, to die one by one until none are left.

Seth Morley beckoned him off to one side, away from the others. 'You're sure you don't want to tell them? They have a right to know who the enemy is.'

Belsnor said, 'I don't want them to know because as I explained to you their morale is low enough already. If they knew it came from Terra they wouldn't be able to survive; they'd go friggin' mad.'

'I'll leave it up to you,' Seth Morley said. 'You've been elected as the group's leader.' But his tone of voice showed that he disagreed, and very strongly. As he had last night.

'In time,' Belsnor said, clamping his long, expert fingers around Seth's upper arm. 'When the right time comes—'

'It never will,' Seth Morley said, moving back a step. 'They'll die without knowing.'

Maybe, Belsnor thought, it would be better that way. Better if all men, wherever they are, were to die without knowing who did it or why.

Squatting down, Russell turned Susie Smart over; he gazed down at her and said, 'She certainly was a pretty girl.'

'Pretty,' Belsnor said harshly, 'but batty. She had an overactive sex drive; she had to sleep with every man she came across. We can do without her.'

'You bastard,' Seth Morley said, his tone fierce.

Belsnor lifted his empty hands and said, 'What do you want me to say? That we can't get along without her? That this is the end?'

Morley did not answer.

To Maggie Walsh, Belsnor said, 'Say a prayer.' It was time for the ceremony of death, the rituals so firmly attached to it that even he himself could not imagine a death without it.

'Give me a few minutes,' Maggie Walsh said huskily. 'I – just can't talk now.' She retreated and turned her back; he heard her sobbing.

'I'll say it,' Belsnor said, with savage fury.

Seth Morley said, 'I'd like permission to go on an exploratory trip outside the settlement. Russell wants to come along.'

'Why?' Belsnor said.

Morley said in a low, steady voice, 'I've seen the miniaturized version of the Building. I think it's time to confront the real thing.'

'Take someone with you,' Belsnor said. 'Someone who knows their way around out there.'

'I'll go with them,' Betty Jo Berm spoke up.

'There should be another man with them,' Belsnor said. But he thought, it's a mistake for us not to stay together; death comes when one of us is off by himself. 'Take Frazer and Thugg, both of them, with you,' he decided. 'As well as B.J.' That would split the group, but neither Roberta Rockingham nor Bert Kosler were physically able to make such a journey. Neither had as yet left the camp. 'I'll stay here with the rest of them,' he said.

98

'I think we should be armed,' Wade Frazer said.

'Nobody's going to be armed,' Belsnor said. 'We're in a bad enough situation already. If you're armed you'll kill one another, either accidentally or intentionally.' He did not know why he felt this, but intuitively he knew himself to be correct. Susie Smart, he thought. Maybe you were killed by one of us . . . one who is an agent of Terra and General Treaton.

As in my dream, he thought. The enemy within. Age, deterioration and death. Despite the field-barrier surrounding the settlement. That's what my dream was trying to tell me.

Rubbing at her grief-reddened eyes, Maggie Walsh said, 'I'd like to go along with them.'

'Why?' Belsnor said. 'Why does everyone want to leave the settlement? We're safer here.' But his knowledge, his awareness of the untruth of what he was saying, found its way into his voice; he heard his own insincerity. 'Okay,' he said. 'And good luck.' To Seth Morley he said, 'Try and bring back one of those singing flies. Unless you find something better.'

'I'll do the best I can,' Seth Morley said. Turning, he moved away from Belsnor. Those who were going with him started away, too.

They'll never come back, Belsnor said to himself. He watched them go and, within him, his heart struck heavy, muffled blows, as if the pendulum of the cosmic clock were swinging back and forth, back and forth, within his hollow chest.

The pendulum of death.

The seven of them trudged along the edge of a low ridge, their attention fixed on each object that they saw. They said very little.

Unfamiliar hazy hills spread out, lost in billowing dust. Green lichens grew everywhere; the soil was a tangled floor of growing plants. The air smelled of intricate organic life here. A rich, complex odour, nothing like any of

99

them had smelled before. Off in the distance great columns of steam rose up, geysers of boiling water forcing its way through the rocks to the surface. An ocean lay far off, pounding invisibly in the drifting curtain of dust and moisture.

They came to a damp place. Warm slime, compounded from water, dissolved minerals and fungoid pulp, lapped at their shoes. The remains of lichens and protozoa coloured and thickened the scum of moisture dripping everywhere, over the wet rocks and sponge-like shrubbery.

Bending down, Wade Frazer picked up a snail-like unipedular organism. 'It's not fake – this is alive. It's genuine.'

Thugg was holding a sponge which he had fished from a small, warm pool. 'This is artificial. But there are legitimate sponges like this on Delmak-O. And these are fakes, too.' From the water Thugg grabbed a wriggling snake-like creature with short, stubby legs that thrashed furiously. Swiftly, Thugg removed the head; the head came off and the creature stopped moving. 'A totally mechanical contraption – you can see the wiring.' He restored the head; once more the creature began flopping. Thugg tossed it back in the water and it swam happily off.

'Where's the Building?' Mary Morley said.

Maggie Walsh said, 'It – seems to change locations. The last time anyone encountered it it was along this ridge and past the geysers. But it probably won't be next time.'

'We can use this as a starting stage,' Betty Jo Berm said. 'When we get to the spot where it last was we can fan out in various directions.' She added, 'It's a shame we don't have intercoms with us. They would be a lot of help.'

'That's Belsnor's fault,' Thugg said. 'He's our elected leader; he's supposed to think of technical details like that.'

To Seth Morley Betty Jo Berm said, 'Do you like it out here?'

'I don't know yet.' Perhaps because of Susie Smart's

death he felt repelled by everything he saw. He did not like the mixture of artificial life forms with the real ones; the mixing together of them made him sense the whole landscape as false . . . as if, he thought, those hills in the background, and that great plateau to the right, are a painted backdrop. As if all this, and ourselves, and the settlement – all are contained in a geodetic dome. And above us Treaton's research men, like entirely deformed scientists of pulp fiction, are peering down at us as we walk, tiny-creature-wise, along our humble way.

'Let's stop and rest,' Maggie Walsh said, her face grim and elongated still; the shock of Susie's death had, for her, not worn off in the slightest. 'I'm tired. I didn't have any breakfast, and we didn't bring any food with us. This whole trip should have been carefully planned out in advance.'

'None of us were thinking clearly,' Betty Jo Berm said with sympathy. She brought a bottle out of her skirt pocket, opened it, sorted among the pills and at last found one that was satisfactory.

'Can you swallow those without water?' Russell asked her.

'Yes,' she said, and smiled. 'A pillhead can swallow a pill under any circumstances.'

Seth Morley said to Russell, 'For B.J. it's pills.' He eyed Russell, wondering about him. Like the others, did this new member also have a weak link in his character? And if so, what was it?

'I think I know what Mr Russell's fondness is for,' Wade Frazer said in his somewhat nasty, baiting voice. 'He has, I believe, from what I've observed about him, a cleaning fetish.'

'Really?' Mary Morley said.

'I'm afraid so,' Russell said and smiled to show perfect, white teeth, like the teeth of an actor.

They continued on and came, at last, to a river. It seemed too wide to cross; there they halted.

'We'll have to follow the river,' Thugg said. He scowled. 'I've been in this area, but I didn't see any river before.'

Frazer giggled and said, 'It's for you, Morley. Because you're a marine biologist.'

Maggie Walsh said, 'That's a strange remark. Do you mean the landscape alters according to our expectation?'

'I was making a joke,' Frazer said insultingly.

'But what a strange idea,' Maggie Walsh said. 'You know, Specktowsky speaks about us as being "prisoners of our own preconceptions and expectations". And that one of the conditions of the Curse is to remain mired in the quasi-reality of those proclivities. Without ever seeing reality as it actually is.'

'Nobody sees reality as it actually is,' Frazer said. 'As Kant proved. Space and time are modes of perception, for example. Did you know that?' He poked at Seth Morley. 'Did you know that, mister marine biologist?'

'Yes,' he answered, although in point of fact he had never even heard of Kant, much less read him.

'Specktowsky says that ultimately we can see reality as it is,' Maggie Walsh said. 'When the Intercessor releases us from our world and condition. When the Curse is lifted from us, through him.'

Russell spoke up. 'And sometimes, even during our physical lifetime, we get momentary glimpses of it.'

'Only if the Intercessor lifts the veil for us,' Maggie Walsh said.

'True,' Russell admitted.

'Where are you from?' Seth Morley asked Russell.

'From Alpha Centauri 8.'

'That's a long way from here,' Wade Frazer said.

'I know.' Russell nodded. 'That's why I arrived here so late. I'd been travelling for almost three months.'

'Then you were one of the first to obtain a transfer,' Seth Morley said. 'Long before me.'

'Long before any of us,' Wade Frazer said. He contemplated Russell, who stood head and shoulders above him. 'I wonder why an economist would be wanted here. There's no economy on this planet.'

Maggie Walsh said, 'There seems to be no use to which *any* of us can put our skills. Our skills, our training – they don't seem to matter. I don't think we were selected because of them.'

'Obviously,' Thugg grated.

'Is that so obvious to you?' Betty Jo said to him. 'Then what do you think the basis of selection was?'

'Like Belsnor says. We're all misfits.'

'He doesn't say we're misfits,' Seth Morley said. 'He says we're failures.'

'It's the same thing,' Thugg said. 'We're the debris of the galaxy. Belsnor is right, for once.'

'Don't include me when you say that,' Betty Jo said. 'I'm not willing to admit I'm part of the "debris of the universe" quite yet. Maybe tomorrow.'

'As we die,' Maggie Walsh said, half to herself, 'we sink into oblivion. An oblivion in which we already exist . . . one out of which only the Deity can save us.'

'So we have the Deity trying to save us,' Seth Morley said, 'and General Treaton trying to—' He broke off; he had said too much. But no one noticed.

'That's the basic condition of life anyhow,' Russell put in, in his neutral, mild voice. 'The dialectic of the universe. One force pulling us down to death; the Form Destroyer in all his manifestations. Then the Deity in His three Manifestations. Theoretically always at our elbow. Right, Miss Walsh?'

'Not theoretically.' She shook her head. 'Actually.'

Betty Jo Berm said quietly, 'There's the Building.'

So now he saw it. Seth Morley shaded his eyes against the bright midday sun, peered. Grey and large, it reared up at the limit of his vision. A cube, almost. With odd spires . . . probably from heat-sources. From the machinery and

103

activity within. A pall of smoke hung over it and he thought, It's a factory.

'Let's go,' Thugg said, starting in that direction.

They trudged that way, strung out in an uneven file.

'It's not getting any closer,' Wade Frazer said presently, with jejune derision.

'Walk faster then,' Thugg said with a grin.

'It won't help.' Maggie Walsh halted, gasping. Circles of dark sweat were visible about her armpits. 'Always it's like this. You walk and walk and it recedes and recedes.'

'And you never get really close,' Wade Frazer said. He too, had stopped walking; he was busy lighting up a battered rosewood pipe . . . using with it, Seth Morley noted, one of the worst and strongest pipe-mixtures in existence. The smell of it, as the pipe flared into irregular burning, befouled the natural air.

'Then what do we do?' Russell said.

'Maybe you can think of something,' Thugg said. 'Maybe if we close our eyes and walk around in a little circle we'll find ourselves standing next to it.'

'As we stand here,' Seth Morley said, shading his eyes and peering, 'it gets closer.' He was positive. He could pick out all the spires now, and the pall of smoke above it seemed to have lifted. Maybe it's not a factory after all, he thought. *If it will come just a little nearer maybe I can tell.* He peered on and on; the others, presently, did the same.

Russell said reflectively, 'It's a phantasm. A projection of some kind. From a transmitter located probably within a square mile of us. A very efficient, modern vidtransmitter . . . but you can still see a slight waver.'

'What do you suggest, then?' Seth Morley asked him. 'If you're right then there's no reason to try to get close to it, since it isn't there.'

'It's somewhere,' Russell corrected. 'But not in that spot. What we're seeing is a fake. But there is a real Building and it probably is not far off.'

'How can you know that?' Seth Morley said.

Russell said, 'I'm familiar with Interplan West's method of decoy-composition. This illusory transmission is in existence to fool those who know there is a Building. Who expect to find it. And when they see this they think they have. This is not for someone who does not know there is a Building somewhere out here.' He added, 'This worked very well in the war between Interplan West and the warrior-cults of Rigel 10. Rigelian missiles zeroed in on illusory industrial complexes over and over again. You see, this kind of projection shows up on radar screens and computerized sweep-scanner probes. It has a kind of semi-material basis; strictly speaking it's not a mirage.'

'Well, you would know,' Betty Jo Berm said. 'You're an economist; you'd be familiar with what happened to industrial complexes during a war.' But she did not sound convinced.

'Is that why it retreats?' Seth Morley asked him. 'As we approach?'

'That is how I made out its composition,' Russell said.

Maggie Walsh said to him, 'Tell us what to do.'

'Let's see.' Russell sighed, pondered. The others waited. 'The real Building could be almost anywhere. There's no way to trace it back from the phantasm; if there were, the method would not have worked. I think—' He pointed. 'I have a feeling that the plateau over there is illusory. A superimposition over something, resulting in a negative hallucination for anyone who sights in that direction.' He explained, 'A negative hallucination – when you do not see something that's actually there.'

'Okay,' Thugg said. 'Let's head for the plateau.'

'That means crossing the river,' Mary Morley said.

To Maggie Walsh, Frazer said, 'Does Specktowsky say anything about walking on water? It would be useful, right now. That river looks damn deep to me, and we already decided we couldn't take the chance of trying to cross it.'

'The river may not be there either,' Seth Morley said.

'It's there,' Russell said. He walked towards it, stopped at its edge, bent down and lifted out a temporary handful of water.

'Seriously,' Betty Jo Berm said, 'does Specktowsky say anything about walking on water?'

'It can be done,' Maggie Walsh said, 'but only if the person or persons are in the presence of the Deity. The Deity would have to lead him – or them – across; otherwise they'd sink and drown.'

Ignatz Thugg said, 'Maybe Mr Russell is the Deity.' To Russell he said, 'Are you a Manifestation of the Deity? Come here to help us? Are you, specifically, the Walker-on-Earth?'

'Afraid not,' Russell said in his reasonable, neutral voice.

'Lead us across the water,' Seth Morley said to him.

'I can't,' Russell said. 'I'm a man just like you.'

'Try,' Seth Morley said.

'It's strange,' Russell said, 'that you would think I'm the Walker-on-Earth. It's happened before. Probably because of the nomadic existence I lead. I'm always showing up as a stranger, and if I do anything right – which is rare – then someone gets the bright idea that I'm the third Manifestation of the Deity.'

'Maybe you are,' Seth Morley said, scrutinizing him keenly; he tried to recall how the Walker-on-Earth had looked when he had revealed himself back at Tekel Upharsin. There was little resemblance. And yet – the odd intuition, to an extent, remained with him. It had come to him with no warning: one moment he had accepted Russell as an ordinary man and then all at once he had felt himself to be in the presence of the Deity. And it lingered; it did not completely go away.

'I'd know if I was,' Russell pointed out.

'Maybe you do know,' Maggie Walsh said. 'Maybe Mr Morley is right.' She, too, scrutinized Russell, who looked

106

now a little embarrassed. 'If you are,' she said, 'we will know eventually.'

'Have you ever seen the Walker?' Russell asked her.

'No.'

'I am not he,' Russell said.

'Let's just wade into the goddam water and see if we can make the other side,' Thugg said impatiently. 'If it's too deep then the hell with it; we'll turn back. Here I go.' He strode toward the river and into it; his legs disappeared in the opaque blue-grey water. He continued on and, by degrees, the others followed after him.

They reached the far side with no trouble. All across, the river remained shallow. Feeling chagrined the six of them – and Russell – stood together, slapping water from their clothing. It had come up to their waists and no further.

'Ignatz Thugg,' Frazer said. 'Manifestation of the Deity. Equipped to ford rivers and battle typhoons. I never guessed.'

'Up yours,' Thugg said.

To Maggie Walsh, Russell said suddenly, 'Pray.'

'For what?'

'For the veil of illusion to rise to expose the reality beneath.'

'May I do it silently?' she asked. Russell nodded. 'Thank you,' she said, and turned her back to the group; she stood for a time, hands folded, her head bowed, and then she turned back. 'I did as well as I could,' she informed them. She looked happier, now, Seth Morley noticed. Maybe, temporarily, she had forgotten about Susie Smart.

A tremendous pulsation throbbed nearby.

'I can hear it,' Seth Morley said, and felt fear. Enormous, instinctive fear.

A hundred yards away a grey wall rose up into the smoky haze of the midday sky. Pounding, vibrating, the wall creaked as if alive . . . while, above it, spires squirted wastes in the form of dark clouds. Further wastes, from enormous pipes, gurgled into the river. Gurgled and gurgled and never ceased.

They had found the Building.

NINE

'So now we can see it,' Seth Morley said. At last. It makes a noise, he thought, like a thousand cosmic babies dropping an endless number of giant pot lids on to a titanic concrete floor. What are they doing in there? he asked himself, and started toward the front face of the structure, to see what was inscribed over the entrance.

'Noisy, isn't it?' Wade Frazer shouted.

'Yes,' he said, and was unable to hear his own voice over the stupendous racket of the Building.

He followed a paved road that led along the side of the structure; the others tagged after him, some of them holding their ears. Now he came out in front, shielded his eyes and peered up, focused on the raised surface above the closed sliding doors.

WINERY

That much noise from a winery? he asked himself. It makes no sense.

A small door bore a sign reading: Customers' entrance to wine and cheese tasting room. Holy smoke, he said to himself, the thought of cheese drifting through his mind and burnishing all the shiny parts of his conscious attention. I ought to go in, he said to himself. Apparently it's free, although they like you to buy a couple of bottles before you leave. But you don't have to.

Too bad, he thought, that Ben Tallchief isn't here.

With his great interest in alcoholic beverages this would constitute, for him, a fantastic discovery.

'Wait!' Maggie Walsh called from behind him. 'Don't go in!'

His hand on the customers' door, he half-turned, wondering what was the matter.

Maggie Walsh peeped up into the splendour of the sun and saw mixed with its remarkably strong rays a glimmer of words. She traced the letters with her finger, trying to stabilize them. What does it say? she asked herself. What message does it have for us, with all we yearn to know?

WITTERY

'Wait!' she called to Seth Morley, who stood with his hand on a small door marked: Customers' entrance. 'Don't go in!'

'Why not?' he yelled back.

'We don't know what it is!' She came breathlessly up beside him. The great structure shimmered in the mobile sunlight which spilled and dribbled over its higher surfaces. As if one could walk upon a single mote, she said to herself longingly. A carrier to the universal self: made partly of this world, partly of the next. *Wittery.* A place where knowledge is accumulated? But it made too much noise to be a book and tape and microfilm depository. Where witty conversations take place? Perhaps the essences of man's wit were being distilled within; she might find herself immersed in the wit of Dr Johnson, of Voltaire.

But wit did not mean humour. It meant perspicacity. It meant the most fundamental form of intelligence coupled with a certain amount of grace. But, over all, the capacity of man to possess absolute knowledge.

If I go in there, she thought, I will learn all that man can know in this interstice of dimensions. I must go in. She hurried up to Seth Morley, nodding. 'Open the door,' she said. 'We must go inside the wittery; we've got to learn what is in there.'

Ambling after them, regarding their agitation with distinguished irony, Wade Frazer perceived the legend incised above the closed, vast doors of the Building.

At first he was perplexed. He could decipher the letters and thus make out the word. But he had not the foggiest notion as to the meaning of the word.

'I don't get it,' he said to Seth Morley and the religious fanatic of the colony, Mag the Hag. He strained once more to see, wondering if his problem lay in a psychological ambivalence; perhaps on some lower level he did not really desire to know what the letters spelled. So he had garbled it, to foil his own manoeuvring.

STOPPERY

Wait, he thought, I think I know what a stoppery is. It is based on the Celtic, I believe. A dialect word only comprehensible to someone who has a varied and broad background of liberal, humanistic information at his disposal. Other persons would walk right by.

It is, he thought, a place where deranged persons are apprehended and their activities curtailed. In a sense it's a sanatorium, but it goes much further than that. The aim is not to cure the ill and then return them to society – probably as ill as they ever were – but to close the final door on man's ignorance and folly. Here, at this point, the deranged preoccupations of the mentally ill come to an end; they *stop*, as the incised sign reads. They – the mentally ill who come here – are not returned to society, they are quietly and painlessly put to sleep. Which, ultimately, must be the fate of all who are incurably sick. Their poisons must not continue to contaminate the galaxy, he said to himself. Thank God there is such a place as this; I wonder why I wasn't notified of it *vis-à-vis* the trade journals.

I must go in, he decided. I want to see how they work. And let's find out what their legal basis is; there remains, after all, the sticky problem of the nonmedical authorities – if they could be called that – intervening and blocking the process of stoppery.

'Don't go in!' he yelled at Seth Morley and the religious nut Maggie Baggie. 'This isn't for you; it's probably classified. Yes. See?' He pointed to the legend on the small aluminium door; it read: Trained personnel entrance only. 'I can go in!' he yelled at them over the din, 'but you can't! You're not qualified!' Both Maggie Baggie Haggie and Seth Morley looked at him in a startled way, but stopped. He pushed past them.

Without difficulty, Mary Morley perceived the writing over the entrance of the grey, large building.

WITCHERY

I know what it is, she said to herself, but they don't. A witchery is a place where the control of people is exercised by means of formulas and incantations. Those who rule are masters because of their contact with the witchery and its brew, its drugs.

'I'm going in there,' she said to her husband.

Seth said, 'Wait a minute. Just hold on.'

'I can go in,' she said, 'but you can't. It's there for me. I know it. I don't want you to stop me; get out of the way.'

She stood before the small door, reading the gold letters that adhered to the glass. Introductory chamber open to all qualified visitors, the door read. Well, that means me, she thought. It's speaking directly to me. That's what it means by 'qualified.'

'I'll go in with you,' Seth said.

Mary Morley laughed. Go in with her? Amusing, she thought; he thinks they'll welcome him in the witchery. A

111

man. This is only for women, she said to herself; there aren't any male witches.

After I've been in there, she realized, I'll know things by which I can control him; I can make him into what he ought to be, rather than what he is. So in a sense I'm doing it for his sake.

She reached for the knob of the door.

Ignatz Thugg stood off to one side, chuckling to see their antics. They howled and bleated like pigs. He felt like walking up and sticking them but who cared? I'll bet they stink when you get right up close to them, he told himself. They look so clean and underneath they stink. What is this poop place? He squinted, trying to read the jerky letters.

HIPPERY HOPPERY

Hey, he said to himself. That's swell; that's where they have people hop on to animals for youknowwhat. I always wanted to watch a horse and a woman make it together; I bet I can see that inside there. Yeah; I really want to see that, for everyone to watch. They show everything really good in there and like it really is.

And there'll be real people watching who I can talk to. Not like Morley and Walsh and Frazer using fatass words that're so long they sound like farting. They use words like that to make it look like their poop don't stink. But they're no different from me.

Maybe, he thought, they have fat asses, people like Babble, making it with big dogs. I'd like to see some of these fatassed people in there plugging away; I'd like to see that Walsh plugged by a Great Dane for once in her life. She'd probably love that. That's what she really wants out of life; she probably dreams about it.

'Get out of the way,' he said to Morley and Walsh and Frazer. 'You can't go in there. Look at what it says.' He pointed to the words painted in classy gold on the glass window of the small door. Club members only. 'I can go in,' he said, and reached for the knob.

Going swiftly forward, Ned Russell interposed himself between them and the door. He glanced up at the class-one building, saw then on their various faces separate and intense cravings, and he said, 'I think it would be better if none of us goes in.'

'Why?' Seth Morley said, visibly disappointed. 'What could be harmful in going into the tasting room of a winery?'

'It's not a winery,' Ignatz Thugg said, and chortled with glee. 'You read it wrong; you're afraid to admit what it really is.' He chortled once again. 'But *I* know.'

'Winery!' Maggie Walsh exclaimed. 'It's not a winery, it's a symposium of the achievement of man's highest knowledge. If we go in there we'll be purified by God's love for man and man's love for God.'

'It's a special club for certain people only,' Thugg said.

Frazer said, with a smirk, 'Isn't it amazing, the lengths people will go to in an unconscious effort to block their having to face reality. Isn't that correct, Russell?'

Russell said, 'It's not safe in there. For any of us.' I know now what it is, he said to himself, and I am right. I must get them – and myself – away from here. 'Go,' he said to them, forcefully and sternly. He remained there, not budging.

Some of their energy faded.

'You think so, really?' Seth Morley said.

'Yes,' he said. 'I think so.'

To the others, Seth Morley said, 'Maybe he's right.'

'Do you really think so, Mr Russell?' Maggie Walsh said in a faltering voice. They retreated from the door. Slightly. But enough.

Crushed, Ignatz Thugg said, 'I knew they'd close it down. They don't want anyone to get any kickers out of life. It's always that way.'

Russell said nothing; he stood there, blocking the door, and patiently waiting.

All at once Seth Morley said, 'Where's Betty Jo Berm?'

Merciful God, Russell thought. I forgot her. I forgot to watch. He turned rapidly and, shielding his eyes, peered back the way they had come. Back at the sunlit, midday river.

She had seen again what she had seen before. Each time that she saw the Building she clearly made out the vast bronze plaque placed boldly above the central entrance.

MEKKISRY

As a linguist she had been able to translate it the first time around. *Mekkis*, the Hittite word for power; it had passed into the Sanskrit, then into Greek, Latin, and at last into modern English as *machine* and *mechanical*. This was the place denied her; she could not come here, as the rest of them could.

I wish I were dead, she said to herself.

Here was the font of the universe . . . at least as she understood it. She understood as literally true Specktowsky's theory of concentric circles of widening emanation. But to her it did not concern a Deity; she understood it as a statement of material fact, with no transcendental aspects. When she took a pill she rose, for a brief moment, into a higher, smaller circle of greater intensity and concentration of power. Her body weighed less; her ability, her motions, her animation – all functioned as if powered by a better fuel. I burn better, she said to herself as she turned and walked away from the Building, back toward the river. I am able to think more clearly; I am not clouded over as I am now, drooping under a foreign sun.

The water will help, she said to herself. Because in water you no longer have to support your heavy body; you are not lifted into greater *mekkis* but you do not care; the water erases everything. You are not heavy; you are not light. You are not even there.

I can't go on dragging my heavy body everywhere, she said to herself. The weight is too much. I cannot endure being pulled down any longer; I have to be free.

She stepped into the shallows. And walked out, toward the centre. Without looking back.

The water, she thought, has now dissolved all the pills I carry; they are gone forever. But I no longer have any need for them. If I could enter the *Mekkisry* ... maybe, without a body, I can, she thought. There to be remade. There to cease, and then begin all over. But starting at a different point. I do not want to go over again what I have gone over already, she told herself.

She could hear the vibrating roar of the *Mekkisry* behind her. The others are in there now, she realized. Why, she asked herself, is it this way? *Why can they go where I can't?* She did not know.

She did not care.

'There she is,' Maggie Walsh said, pointing. Her hand shook. 'Can't you see her?' She broke into motion, became unfrozen; she sprinted toward the river. But before she reached it Russell and Seth Morley passed her, leaving her behind. She began to cry, stopped running and stood there, watching through fragmented bits of crystal-like tears as Thugg and Wade Frazer caught up with Seth Morley and Russell; the four men, with Mary Morley trailing after them, rapidly waded out into the river, towards the black object drifting slightly towards the far side.

Standing there, she watched them carry Betty Jo's body from the water and up on to land. She's dead, she realized. While we argued about going into the *Wittery*. Goddam it, she thought brokenly. Then, halting, she made her way toward the five of them who knelt around B.J.'s body, taking turns at giving mouth-to-mouth resuscitation.

She reached them. Stood. 'Any chance?' she said.

'No,' Wade Frazer said.

'Goddam it,' she said, and her voice came out broken and lame. 'Why did she do it? Frazer, do you know?'

'Some pressure that's built up over a long period of time,' Frazer said.

Seth Morley stared at him with violence flaming in his eyes. 'You fool,' he said. 'You stupid bastard fool.'

'It's not my fault she's dead,' Frazer chattered anxiously. 'I didn't have enough testing apparatus to give anyone a really complete exam; if I had had what I wanted I could have uncovered and treated her suicidal tendencies.'

'Can we carry her back to the settlement?' Maggie Walsh said in a tear-stricken voice; she found herself almost unable to speak. 'If you four men could carry her—'

'If we could float her down the river,' Thugg said, 'it'd be a lot less work. By river around half the time is cut off.'

'We have nothing to float her on,' Mary Morley said.

Russell said, 'When we were crossing the river I saw what looked like a jury-rigged raft. I'll show you.' He beckoned them to follow him to the river's edge.

There it lay, trapped into immobility by an extrusion of the river. It lay undulating slightly from the activity of the water, and Maggie Walsh thought, It almost looks as if it's here on purpose. For this reason: to carry one of us who has died back home.

'Belsnor's raft,' Ignatz Thugg said.

'That's right,' Frazer said, picking at his right ear. 'He did say he was building a raft somewhere out here. Yes, you can see how he's lashed the logs together with heavy-duty electric cable. I wonder if it's well enough put together to be safe.'

'If Glen Belsnor built it,' Maggie said fiercely, 'it's safe. Put her on it.' And in the name of God be gentle, she said to herself. Be reverent. What you're carrying is holy.

The four men, grunting, instructing one another as to

what to do and how to do it, managed at last to move the body of Betty Jo Berm on to Belsnor's raft.

She lay face up, her hands placed across her stomach. Her eyes sightlessly fixed on the harsh midday sky. Water dribbled from her still, and her hair seemed to Maggie like some hive of black wasps which had fastened on an adversary, never again to let it go.

Attacked by death, she thought. The wasps of death. And the rest of us, she thought; when will it happen to us? Who will be the next? Maybe me, she thought. Yes, possibly me.

'We can all get on the raft with her,' Russell said. To Maggie he said, 'Do you know at what point we should leave the river?'

'I know,' Frazer said, before she could answer.

'Okay,' Russell said matter-of-factly. 'Let's go.' He guided Maggie and Mary Morley down the riverside and on to the raft; he touched the two women in a gentle manner, an attitude of chivalry which Maggie had not encountered in some time.

'Thank you,' she said to him.

'Look at it,' Seth Morley said, gazing back at the Building. The artificial background had already begun to phase into being; the Building wavered, real as it was. As the raft moved out into the river – pushed there by the four men – Maggie saw the huge grey wall of the Building fade into the far-off bronze of a counterfeit plateau.

The raft picked up speed as it entered the central current of the river. Maggie, seated by Betty Jo's wet body, shivered in the sun and shut her eyes. Oh God, she thought, help us get back to the settlement. Where is this river taking us? she asked herself. I've never seen it before; as far as I know it doesn't run near the settlement. We didn't walk along it to get here. Aloud, she said. 'Why do you think this river will take us home? I think you've all taken leave of your senses.'

'We can't carry her,' Frazer said. 'It's too far.'

'But this is taking us farther and farther away,' Maggie said. She was positive of it. 'I want to get off!' she said, and scrambled to her feet in panic. The raft was moving too swiftly; she felt trapped fear as she saw the contours of the banks passing in such quick succession.

'Don't jump into the water,' Russell said, taking her by the arm. 'You'll be all right; we'll all be all right.'

The raft continued to gather speed. Now no one spoke; they rode along quietly, feeling the sun, sensing the water . . . and all of them afraid and sobered by what had happened. And, Maggie Walsh thought, by what lies ahead.

'How did you know about the raft?' Seth Morley asked Russell.

'As I said, I saw it when we—'

'Nobody else saw it,' Seth Morley broke in.

Russell said nothing.

'Are you a man or are you a Manifestation?' Seth Morley said.

'If I was a Manifestation of the Deity I would have saved her from drowning,' Russell pointed out caustically. To Maggie Walsh he said, 'Do you think I'm a Manifestation?'

'No,' she said. How I wish you were, she thought. How badly we need intercession.

Bending, Russell touched Betty Jo Berm's black, dead, soaked hair. They continued on in silence.

Tony Dunkelwelt, shut up in his hot room, sat cross-legged on the floor and knew that he had killed Susie.

My miracle, he thought. It must have been the Form Destroyer who came when I called. It turned the bread into stone and then took the stone from her and killed her with it. The stone I made. No matter how you look at it, it goes back to me.

Listening, he heard no sound. Half the group had gone;

the remaining half had sunk into oblivion. Maybe they're all gone now, he said to himself. I'm alone . . . left here to fall into the terrible paws of the Form Destroyer.

'I will take the Sword of Chemosh,' he said aloud. 'And slay the Form Destroyer with it.' He held up his hand, groping for the Sword. He had seen it before during his meditations, but he had never touched it. 'Give me the Sword of Chemosh,' he said, 'and I will do its work; I will seek out the Black One and murder it forever. It will never rise again.'

He waited but saw nothing.

'Please,' he said. And then he thought, I must merge more deeply into the universal self. I am still separate. He shut his eyes and compelled his body to relax. Receive, he thought; I must be clear enough and empty enough to have it pour into me. Once again I must be a hollow vessel. As so many, many times before.

But he could not do it now.

I am impure, he realized. So they send me nothing. By what I have done I've lost the capacity to accept and even to see. Will I never see the God-Above-God again? he asked himself. Has it all ended?

My punishment, he thought.

But I don't deserve it. Susie wasn't that important. She was demented; the stone left her in revulsion. That was it; the stone was pure and she was impure. But still, he thought, it's awful that she's dead. Brightness, mobility and light – Susie had all three. But it was a broken, fractured light which she gave off. A light which scorched and injured . . . me, for example. It was wrong for me. What I did I did in self-defence. It's obvious.

'The Sword,' he said. 'The Sword-wrath of Chemosh. Let it come to me.' He rocked back and forth, reached up once again into the awesomeness above him. His hand groped, disappeared; he watched it as it vanished. His fingers fumbled in empty space, a million miles into emptiness, the hollowness above man . . . he continued to grope on and on, and then, abruptly, his fingers touched something.

Touched – but did not grasp.

I swear, he said to himself, that if I am given the Sword I will use it. I will avenge her death.

Again he touched but did not grasp. I know it is there, he thought; I can feel it with my fingers. 'Give it to me!' he said aloud. 'I swear that I'll use it!' He waited, and then, into his empty hand, was placed something hard, heavy and cold.

The Sword. He held it.

He drew the Sword downward, carefully. God-like, it blazed with heat and light; it filled the room with its authority. He at once leaped up, almost dropping the Sword. I have it now, he said to himself joyfully. He ran to the door of the room, the Sword wobbling in his meagre grip. Pushing open the door he emerged in the midday light; gazing around he said, 'Where are you, mighty Form Destroyer, you decayer of life? Come and fight with me!'

A shape moved clumsily, slowly along the porch. A bent shape which crept blindly, as if accustomed to the darkness within the Earth. It looked up at him with filmed-over grey eyes; he saw and understood the shirt of dust which clung to it . . . dust trickled silently down it's bent body and drifted into the air. And it left a fine trail of dust as it moved.

It was badly decayed. Yellowed, wrinkled skin covered its brittle bones. Its cheeks were sunken and it had no teeth. The Form Destroyer hobbled forward, seeing him; as it hobbled it wheezed to itself and squeaked a few wretched words. Now its dry-skin hand groped for him and it rasped, 'Hey there, Tony. Hey there. How are you?'

'Are you coming to meet me?' he said.

'Yes,' it gasped, and came a step closer. He smelled it, now; a mixture of fungus-breath and the rot of centuries. It did not have long to live. Plucking at him it cackled; saliva ran down its chin and dripped on to the floor. It tried to wipe the saliva away with the crust-like back of its hand, but could not. 'I want you—' it started to say, and then he stuck the Sword of Chemosh into its paunchy, soft middle.

Handfuls of worms, white pulpy worms, oozed out of it as he withdrew the Sword. Again it laughed its dry cackle; it stood there swaying, one arm and hand groping for him . . . he stepped back and looked away as the worms grew in a pile before it. It had no blood: it was a sack of corruption and nothing more.

It sank down on to one knee, still cackling. Then, in a kind of convulsion, it clawed at its hair. Between its grasping fingers strands of long, lustreless hair appeared; it tore the hair from itself, then held it in his direction, as if it meant to give him something priceless.

He stabbed it again. Now it lay, sightlessly; its eyes gummed over entirely and its mouth fell open.

From its mouth a single furry organism, like an inordinately large spider, crawled. He stepped on it and, under his foot, it lay mashed into oblivion.

I have killed the Form Destroyer, he said.

From far off, on the other side of the compound, a voice carried to him. '*Tony!*' A shape came running. At first he could not tell who or what it was; he shielded his eyes from the sun and strained to see.

Glen Belsnor. Running as fast as he could.

'I killed the Form Destroyer,' Tony said as Belsnor dashed up on to the porch, his chest heaving. 'See?' He pointed, with his Sword, at the crippled shape lying between them; it had drawn up its legs and entered, at the moment of its death, a foetal position.

'That's Bert Kosler!' Belsnor shouted, panting for breath. 'You killed an old man!'

'No,' he said, and looked down. He saw Bert Kosler, the settlement's custodian, lying there. 'He fell into the possession of the Form Destroyer,' he said, but he did not believe it – he saw what he had done, knew what he had done.

'I'm sorry,' he said. 'I'll ask the God-Above-God to bring
him back.' He turned and ran into his room; locking the
door he stood there shaking. Nausea flung itself up into his
throat; he gagged, blinked . . . deep pains filled his stomach and he had to bend over, groaning with pain. The
Sword fell heavily from him, on to the floor; its clank
frightened him and he retreated a few steps, leaving it to
lie there.

'Open the door!' Glen Belsnor yelled from outside.

'No,' he said, and his teeth chattered; terrible cold
dashed through his arms and legs; the cold knotted itself
into the nausea in his stomach, and the pains became
greater.

At the door a terrible crash sounded; the door hesitated
and creaked, then abruptly threw itself open.

Glen Belsnor stood there, grey-haired and grim, holding
a military pistol pointed directly into the room. Directly
at Tony Dunkelwelt.

Bending, Tony Dunkelwelt reached to pick up the
Sword.

'Don't,' Glen Belsnor said, 'or I'll kill you.'

His hand closed over the handle of the Sword.

Glen Belsnor fired at him. Point-blank.

TEN

As the raft drifted downstream, Ned Russell stood staring
off in the distance, cloaked by his own thoughts.

'What are you looking for?' Seth Morley asked him.

Russell pointed. 'There, I see one.' He turned to
Maggie. 'Isn't that one of them?'

'Yes,' she said. 'The Grand Tench. Or else one almost as
large as he.'

'What kind of questions have you asked them?' Russell said.

Showing surprise, Maggie said, 'We don't ask them anything; we have no way of communicating with them – they don't have a language or vocal organs insofar as we can determine.'

'Telepathically?' Russell said.

'They're not telepathic,' Wade Frazer said. 'And neither are we. All they do is print duplicates of objects . . . which puddle in a few days.'

'They can be communicated with,' Russell said. 'Let's steer this raft over into the shallows; I want to consult with your tench.' He slid from the raft, into the water. 'All of you get off and help me guide it.' He seemed determined; his face was relatively firm. So, one by one, they slid into the water, leaving only B.J.'s silent body aboard the raft.

In a matter of minutes they had pushed the raft up against the grass-covered shore. They moored it firmly – by shoving it deep into the grey mud – and then crawled up on to the bank.

The cube of gelatinous mass towered over them as they approached it. The sunlight danced in a multitude of flecks, as if caught within it. The interior of the organism glowed with activity.

It's bigger than I expected, Seth Morley said to himself. It looks – ageless. How long do they live? he wondered.

'You put articles in front of it,' Ignatz Thugg said, 'and it pushes a hunk of itself out, and then that hunk forms into a duplicate. Here, I'll show you.' He tossed his wet wristwatch on to the ground before the tench. 'Duplicate that, you jello,' he said.

The gelatin undulated, and presently, as Thugg had predicted, a section of it oozed out to come to rest beside the watch. The colour of the production altered; it became silver-like. And then it flattened. Design appeared in the silver-substance. Several more minutes passed, as if the tench were resting, and then all at once the excreted product sank into the shape of a leather-bound disc. It looked exactly like the true watch beside it . . . or rather almost exactly, Seth Morley noted. It was not as bright; it had a dulled quality. But – it was still basically a success.

Russell seated himself in the grass and began to search through his pockets. 'I need a dry piece of paper,' he said.

'I have some in my purse that're still dry,' Maggie Walsh said. She rummaged in her purse, handed him a small pad. 'Do you need a pen?'

'I've got a pen.' He wrote darkly on the top sheet of paper. 'I'm asking it questions.' He finished writing, held the sheet of paper up, and read from it. ' "How many of us will die here at Delmak-O?" ' He folded the paper and placed it before the tench, next to the two wristwatches.

More of the tench's gelatin burbled out, to come to rest in a mound beside Russell's piece of paper.

'Won't it simply duplicate the question?' Seth Morley asked.

'I don't know,' Russell said. 'We'll see.'

Thugg said, 'I think you're barmy.'

Eyeing him, Russell said, 'You have a strange idea, Thugg, of what's "barmy" and what isn't.'

'Is that meant to be an insult?' Thugg flushed an angry red.

Maggie Walsh said, 'Look. The duplicate piece of paper is forming.'

Two folded sheets of paper rested directly in front of the tench. Russell waited a moment, then, evidently deciding that the duplicating process had finished, took the two sheets, unfolded both of them, studied them for a long time.

'Did it answer?' Seth Morley said. 'Or did it repeat the question?'

'It answered.' Russell handed him one of the sheets of paper.

The note was short and simple. And impossible to misinterpret. *You will go out on to your compound and not see your people.*

'Ask it who our enemy is,' Seth Morley said.

'Okay.' Russell wrote again, placed the sheet of paper, folded, before the tench. ' "Who is our enemy?" ' he said. 'That's so to speak the ultimate question.'

The tench fashioned an answering slip, which Russell at once grabbed. He studied it intently, then read it aloud. *'Influential circles.'*

'That doesn't tell us much,' Maggie Walsh said.

Russell said, 'Evidently that's all it knows.'

'Ask it, "What should we do?" ' Seth Morley said.

Russell wrote that, again placing the question before the tench. Presently he had the answer; again he prepared to read aloud. 'This is a long one,' he said apologetically.

'Good,' Wade Frazer said. 'Considering the nature of the question.'

Russell read, *'There are secret forces at work, leading together those who belong together. We must yield to this attraction; then we make no mistakes.'* He pondered. 'We shouldn't have split up; the seven of us shouldn't have left the settlement. If we had stayed there Miss Berm would still be alive. It's obvious that from now on we must keep one another in visual sight all the—' He broke off. An additional glob of gelatin was extruding from the tench. Like those before, it formed into a folded slip of paper. Russell took it, opened and read it. 'Addressed to you,' he said, and handed it to Seth Morley.

'Often a man feels an urge to unite with others, but the individuals around him have already formed themselves into a group, so that he remains isolated. He should then ally himself with a man who stands nearer to the centre of the group and can help him gain admission to the closed circle.' Seth Morley crumpled up the slip of paper and dropped it on to the ground. 'That would be Belsnor,' he said. 'The man who stands nearer to the centre.' It's true,

he thought; I am outside and isolated. But in a sense all of us are. Even Belsnor.

'Maybe it means me,' Russell said.

'No,' Seth Morley said. 'It's Glen Belsnor.'

Wade Frazer said, 'I have a question.' He held out his hand and Russell passed him the pen and paper. Frazer wrote rapidly, then, finished, read them his question. ' "Who or what is the man calling himself Ned Russell?" ' He placed that question in front of the tench.

When the answer appeared, Russell took it. Smoothly and without effort; one moment it lay there and the next he had it in his hand. Calmly, he read it to himself. Then, at last, he passed it to Seth Morley and said, 'You read it aloud.'

Seth Morley did so. *'Every step, forward or backward, leads into danger. Escape is out of the question. The danger comes because one is too ambitious.'* He handed the slip over to Wade Frazer.

'It doesn't tell us a damn thing,' Ignatz Thugg said.

'It tells us that Russell is creating a situation in which every move is a losing move,' Wade Frazer said. 'Danger is everywhere and we can't escape. And the cause is Russell's ambition.' He eyed Russell long and searchingly. 'What's your ambition all about? And why are you deliberately leading us into danger?'

Russell said. 'It doesn't say I'm leading you into danger, it just says that the danger exists.'

'What about your ambition? It's plainly referring to you.'

'The only ambition I have,' Russell said, is to be a competent economist, doing useful work. That's why I asked for a work-transfer; the job I was doing – through no fault of my own – was insipid and worthless. That's why I was so glad to be transferred here to Delmak-O.' He added, 'My opinion has somewhat changed since I arrived here.'

'So has ours,' Seth Morley said.

'Okay,' Frazer said fussily. 'We've learned a little from

the tench but not much. All of us will be killed.' He smiled a mirthless, bitter smile. 'Our enemy is "influential circles". We must stay in close proximity to one another, otherwise they'll knock us off one by one.' He pondered. 'And we're in danger, from every direction; nothing we can do will change that. And Russell is a hazard to us, due to his ambition.' He turned toward Seth Morley and said. 'Have you noticed how he's already taken over as leader of the six of us? As if it's natural to him.'

'It is natural to me,' Russell said.

'So the tench is right,' Frazer said.

After a pause, Russell nodded. 'I suppose so, yes. But someone has to lead.'

'When we get back,' Seth Morley said, 'will you resign and accept Glen Belsnor as the group's leader?'

'If he's competent.'

Frazer said, 'We've elected Glen Belsnor. He's our leader whether you like it or not.'

'But,' Russell said, 'I didn't get a chance to vote.' He smiled. 'So I don't consider myself bound by it.'

'I'd like to ask the tench a couple of questions,' Maggie Walsh said. She took the pen and paper and wrote painstakingly. 'I'm asking, "Why are we alive?" ' She placed the paper before the tench and waited.

The answer, when they had obtained it, read:

To be in the fullness of possession and at the height of power.

'Cryptic,' Wade Frazer said. ' "The fullness of possession and the height of power." Interesting. Is that what life's all about?'

Again Maggie wrote. 'I'm now asking, "Is there a God?" ' She placed the slip before the tench and all of them, even Ignatz Thugg, waited tensely.

The answer came.

You would not believe me.

'What's that mean?' Ignatz Thugg said hotly. 'It doesn't mean nothing; that's what it means. Doesn't mean.'

'But it's the truth,' Russell pointed out. 'If it said no, you wouldn't believe it. Would you?' He turned questioningly toward Maggie.

'Correct,' she said.

'And if it said there was?'

'I already believe it.'

Russell, satisfied, said, 'So the tench is right. It makes no difference to any of us what it says in answer to a question like that.'

'But if it said yes,' Maggie said, 'then I could be sure.'

'You are sure,' Seth Morley said.

'Sweet Jesus,' Thugg said. 'The raft is on fire.'

Leaping up they saw flames billowing and leaping; they heard now the crackle of the wood as it heated up, burned, became glowing ash. The six of them sprinted towards the river . . . but, Seth Morley realized, we're too late.

Standing on the bank they watched helplessly; the burning raft had begun to drift out into the centre of the water. It reached the current and, still engulfed by fire, it drifted downstream, became smaller, became, at last, a spark of yellow fire. And then they could no longer see it.

After a time Ned Russell said, 'We shouldn't feel badly. That's the old Norse way of celebrating death. The dead Viking was laid on his shield, on his boat, and the boat was set on fire and sent drifting out to sea.'

Meditating, Seth Morley thought, *Vikings*. A river, and, beyond it, a mystifying building. The river would be the Rhein and the Building would be Walhalla. That would explain why the raft, with Betty Jo Berm's body on it, caught fire and drifted away. Eerie, he thought, and shivered.

'What's the matter?' Russell asked, seeing his face.

'For a moment,' he said, 'I thought I understood.' But it couldn't be; there had to be another explanation.

The tench, answering questions, would be – he could not remember her name, and then it came to him. Erda.

The goddess of the earth who knew the future. Who answered questions brought to her by Wotan.

And Wotan, he thought, walks among the mortals in disguise. Recognizable only by the fact that he had but one eye. The Wanderer, he is called.

'How's your vision?' he asked Russell. 'Twenty-twenty in both eyes?'

Startled, Russell said, 'No – actually not, as a matter of fact. Why do you ask?'

'One of his eyes is false,' Wade Frazer said. 'I've been noticing. The right one is artificial; it sees nothing, but the muscles operate it, moving it as if it were real.'

'Is that true?' Seth Morley asked.

'Yes.' Russell nodded. 'But it's none of your business.'

And Wotan, Seth Morley recalled, destroyed the gods, brought on *die Götterdämmerung*, by his ambition. What was his ambition? To build the castle of the gods: Walhalla. Well, Walhalla had been built, all right; it bore the legend *Winery*. But it was not a winery.

And, at the end, he thought, it will sink into the Rhein and disappear. And the Rheingold will return to the Rhein Maidens.

But that has not happened yet, he reflected.

Specktowsky had not mentioned *this* in his Book!

Trembling, Glen Belsnor laid the pistol down on the chest of drawers to his right. Before him on the floor, still clutching the great golden sword, lay Tony Dunkelwelt. A tiny flow of blood from his mouth trickled down his cheek and drip-dripped on to the hand-made rug which covered the plastic floor.

Having heard the shot, Dr Babble came running up. Puffing and wheezing he halted at Bert Kosler's body on the porch, turned the withered old body over, examined the sword wound . . . then, seeing Glen Belsnor, he entered the room. Together the two of them stood gazing down.

'I shot him,' Glen Belsnor said. His ears still rang from

the noise of the shot; it had been an ancient lead slug pistol, part of his collection of odds and ends that he carried everywhere he went. He pointed out on to the porch. 'You saw what he did to old Bert.'

'And he was going to stab you, too?' Babble asked.

'Yes.' Glen Belsnor got out his handkerchief and blew his nose; his hand shook and he felt satanically miserable. 'What a hell of a thing,' he said, and heard his voice wobble with grief. 'To kill a kid. But Christ – he would have gotten me, then you, and then Mrs Rockingham.' The thought of anyone killing the distinguished old lady . . . that, more than anything else, had prompted him to act. *He* could have run away; so could Babble. But not Mrs Rockingham.

Babble said, 'Obviously, it was Susie Smart's death that made him psychotic, that brought on his break with reality. He undoubtedly blamed himself for it.' He stooped, picked up the sword. 'I wonder where he got this. I've never seen it before.'

'He always was on the verge of a breakdown,' Glen Belsnor said. 'With those goddam "trances" he went into. He probably heard the voice of God telling him to kill Bert.'

'Did he say anything? Before you killed him?'

' "I killed the Form Destroyer." That's what he said. And then he pointed at Bert's body and said, "See?" Or something like that.' He shrugged weakly. 'Well, Bert was very old. Very much decayed. The handiwork of the Form Destroyer was all over him. God knows. Tony seemed to recognize me. But he was completely insane anyhow. It was all crap he was saying, and then he went for the sword.'

They were both silent for a time.

'Four dead now,' Babble said. 'Maybe more.'

'Why do you say "maybe more"?'

Babble said, 'I'm thinking of those who left the settlement this morning. Maggie, the new man Russell, Seth and Mary Morley—'

'They're probably all right.' But he did not believe his own words. 'No,' he said savagely, 'they're probably all dead. Maybe all seven of them.'

'Try to calm down,' Babble said; he seemed a little afraid. 'Is that gun of yours still loaded?'

'Yes.' Glen Belsnor picked it up, emptied it, handed the shells to Babble. 'You can keep them. No matter what happens I'm not going to shoot anyone else. Not even to save one of the rest of us or all of the rest of us.' He made his way to a chair, seated himself, clumsily got out a cigarette and lit up.

'If there's a court of inquiry,' Babble said, 'I'll be glad to testify that Tony Dunkelwelt was psychiatrically insane. But I can't testify to his killing old Bert, or attacking you. I mean to say, I have only your verbal report for that.' He added quickly, 'But of course I believe you.'

'There won't be any inquiry.' He knew it as an absolute verity; there was no doubt in him on that score. 'Except,' he said, 'a posthumous one. Which won't matter to us.'

'Are you keeping a log of some sort?' Babble asked.

'No.'

'You should.'

'Okay,' he snarled, 'I will. But just leave me alone, goddam it!' He glared at Babble, panting with anger. 'Lay off!'

'Sorry,' Babble said in a small voice, and shrank perceptibly away.

Glen Belsnor said, 'You and I and Mrs Rockingham may be the only ones alive.' He felt it intuitively, in a rush of comprehension.

'Perhaps we should round her up and stay with her. So that nothing happens to her.' Babble cringed his way to the door.

'Okay.' He nodded irritably. 'You know what I'm going to do? You go stay with Mrs Rockingham; I'm going to go over Russell's possessions and his noser. Ever since you and

Morley brought him around last night I've been wondering about him. He seems odd. Did you get that impression?'

'It's just that he's new here.'

'I didn't feel that way about Ben Tallchief. Or the Morleys.' He got abruptly to his feet. 'You know what occurred to me? *Maybe he picked up the aborted signal from the satellite.* I want to get a good look at his transmitter and receiver.' Back to what I know, he pondered. Where I don't feel so alone.

Leaving Babble, he made his way toward the area in which all the nosers lay parked. He did not look back.

The signal from the satellite, he reasoned, short as it was, may have brought him here. He may have been already in the area, not on his way here but preparing a flyby. And yet he had transfer papers. The hell with it, he thought, and began taking apart the radio equipment of Russell's noser.

Fifteen minutes later he knew the answer. Standard receiver and transmitter, exactly like the others in all their other nosers. Russell would not have been able to pick up the satellite's signal because it was a flea-signal. Only the big receiver on Delmak-O could have monitored it. Russell had come in on the automatic pilot, like everybody else. And in the way that everybody else arrived.

So much for that, he said to himself.

Most of Russell's possessions remained aboard the noser; he had only carried his personal articles from the noser to his living quarters. A big box of books. Everybody had books. Glen Belsnor idly tossed the books about, prowling deep in the carton. Textbook after textbook on economics; that figured. Microtapes of several of the great classics, including Tolkien, Milton, Virgil, Homer. All the epics, he realized. Plus *War and Peace,* as well as tapes of John Dos Passos' *U.S.A.* I always meant to read that, he said to himself.

Nothing about the books and tapes struck him as odd. Except—

No copy of Specktowsky's Book.

Maybe Russell, like Maggie Walsh, had memorized it.

Maybe not.

There was one class of people who did not carry a copy of Specktowsky's Book – did not carry it because they were not allowed to read it. The ostriches shut up in the planet-wide aviary at Terra: those who lived in the sandpile because they had crumbled under the enormous psychological pressure suffered while emigrating. Since all the other planets of the Sol System were uninhabitable, emigration meant a trip to another star system . . . and the insidious beginning, for many, of the space illness of loneliness and uprootedness.

Maybe he recovered, Glen Belsnor reflected, and they let him loose. But they then would have made sure he owned a copy of Specktowsky's Book; that would be the time when one really needed it.

He got away, he said to himself.

But why would he come here?

And then he thought, The Interplan West base, where General Treaton operates, is on Terra, tangent to the aviary. What a coincidence. The place, evidently, where all the non-living organisms on Delmak-O had been constructed. As witness the inscription in the tiny replica of the Building.

In a sense it fits together, he decided. But in another sense it adds up to zero. Plain, flat zero.

These deaths, he said to himself, they're making me insane, too. Like they did poor nutty Tony Dunkelwelt. But suppose: a psychological lab, operated by Interplan West, needing aviary patients as subjects. They recruit a batch – those bastards would, too – and one of them is Ned Russell. He's still insane, but they can teach him; the insane can learn, too. They give him a job and send him out to do it – send him here.

And then a gross, vivid, terrifying thought came to him. *Suppose we're all ostriches from the aviary,* he said to himself. Suppose we don't know; Interplan West cut a memory conduit in our friggin' brains. That would explain our inability to function as a group. That's why we can't really even talk clearly to one another. The insane can learn, but one thing they can't do is to function collectively . . . except, perhaps, as a mob. But that is not really functioning in the same sense; that is merely mass insanity.

So we *are* an experiment, then, he thought. I now know what we wanted to know. And it might explain why I have that tattoo stuck away on my right instep, that Persus 9.

But all this was a great deal to base on one slim datum: the fact that Russell did not possess a copy of Specktowsky's Book.

Maybe it's in his goddam living quarters, he thought all at once. Christ, of course; it's *there*.

He departed from the assembly of nosers; ten minutes later he reached the common and found himself stepping up on to the porch. The porch where Susie Smart had died – opposite to the porch where Tony Dunkelwelt and old Bert had died.

We must bury them! he realized – and shrank from it.

But first: I'll look at Russell's remaining stuff.

The door was locked.

With a prybar – taken from his rolypoly aggregate of worldly goods, his great black crowish conglomeration of junk and treasures – he forced open the door.

There, in plain sight, on the rumpled bed, lay Russell's wallet and papers. His transfer, his everything else, back to his birth certificate; Glen Belsnor pawed through them, conscious that here he had something. The chaos attendant on Susie's death had confused them all; undoubtedly Russell had not meant to leave these here. Unless he was not accustomed to carrying them . . . and the ostriches at the aviary did not carry identification of any sort.

At the door appeared Dr Babble. In a voice shrill with panic he said, 'I – can't find Mrs Rockingham.'

'The briefing room? The cafeteria?' She may have gone off for a walk, he thought. But he knew better. Roberta Rockingham could scarcely walk; her cane was essential to her, due to a long-term circulatory ailment. 'I'll help look,' he grunted; he and Babble hurried from the porch and across the common, hiking aimlessly; Glen Belsnor stopped, realizing that they were simply running in fear. 'We have to think,' he gasped. 'Wait a minute.' Where the hell might she be? he asked himself. 'That fine old woman,' he said in frenzy and in despair. 'She never did any harm to anyone in her life. Goddam them, whoever they are.'

Babble nodded glumly.

She had been reading. Hearing a noise, she glanced up. And saw a man, unfamiliar to her, standing in the entranceway of her small, neatly-arranged room.

'Yes?' she said, politely lowering her microtape scanner. 'Are you a new member of the settlement? I haven't seen you before, have I?'

'No, Mrs Rockingham,' he said. His voice was kind and very pleasant, and he wore a leather uniform, complete with huge leather gloves. His face gave off a near radiance ... or perhaps her glasses had steamed up, she wasn't sure. His hair, cut short, did gleam a little, she was positive of that. What a nice expression he has, she declared to herself. So thoughtful, as if he has thought and done many wonderful things.

'Would you like a little bourbon and water?' she asked. Toward afternoon she generally had one drink; it eased the perpetual ache in her legs. Today, however, they could enjoy the Old Crow bourbon a little earlier.

'Thank you,' the man said. Tall, and very slender, he stood at the doorway, not coming fully in. It was as if he were in some way attached to the outside; he could not fully leave it and would soon go back to it entirely. I wonder, she thought, could he be a Manifestation, as the theological people of this enclave call it? She peered at him in an effort to distinguish him more clearly, but the dust on her glasses – or whatever it was – obscured him; she could not get a really clear view.

'I wonder if you might get it,' she said, pointing. 'There's a drawer in that somewhat shabby little table by the bed. You'll find the bottle of Old Crow in there, and three glasses. Oh dear; I don't have any soda. Can you enjoy it with just bottled tapwater? And no ice?'

'Yes,' he said, and walked lightly across her room. He had on tall boots, she observed. How very attractive.

'What is your name?' she inquired.

'Sergeant Ely Nichols.' He opened the table drawer, got out the bourbon and two of the glasses. 'Your colony has been relieved. I was sent here to pick you up and fly you home. From the start they were aware of the malfunctioning of the satellite's tape-transmission.'

'Then it's over?' she said, filled with joy.

'All over,' he said. He filled the two glasses with bourbon and water, brought her hers, seated himself in a straight-backed chair facing her. He was smiling.

ELEVEN

Glen Belsnor, searching futilely for Roberta Rockingham, saw a small number of people trudging toward the settlement. Those who had gone off: Frazer and Thugg, Maggie Walsh, the new man Russell, Mary and Seth Morley . . . they were all there. Or were they?

His heart labouring, Belsnor said, 'I don't see Betty Jo Berm. Is she injured? You left her, you bastards?' He stared at them, feeling his jaw tremble with impotent anger. 'Is that correct?'

'She's dead,' Seth Morley said.

'How?' he said. Dr Babble came up beside him; the two of them waited together as the four men and two women approached.

Seth Morley said, 'She drowned herself.' He looked around. 'Where's that kid, that Dunkelwold?'

'Dead,' Dr Babble said.

Maggie Walsh said, 'And Bert Kosler?'

Neither Babble nor Belsnor answered.

'Then he's dead, too,' Russell said.

'That's right.' Belsnor nodded. 'There're eight of us left. Roberta Rockingham – she's gone. So possibly she's dead, too. I think we'll have to assume she is.'

'Didn't you stay together?' Russell said.

'Did you?' Glen Belsnor answered.

Again there was silence. Somewhere, far off, a warm wind blew dust and infirm lichens about; a swirl lifted above the main buildings of the settlement and then writhed off and was gone. The air, as Glen Belsnor sucked it in noisily, smelled bad. As if, he thought, the skins of dead dogs are drying somewhere on a line.

Death, he thought. That's all I can think of now. And it's easy to see why. Death for us has blotted everything else out; it has become, in less than twenty-four hours, the mainstay of our life.

'You couldn't bring her body back?' he said to them.

'It drifted downstream,' Seth Morley said. 'And it was on fire.' He came up beside Belsnor and said, 'How did Bert Kosler die?'

'Tony stabbed him.'

'What about Tony?'

Glen Belsnor said, 'I shot him. Before he could kill me.'

'What about Roberta Rockingham? Did you shoot her, too?'

'No,' Belsnor said shortly.

'I think,' Frazer said, 'we're going to have to pick a new leader.'

Belsnor said woodenly, 'I had to shoot him. He would have killed all the rest of us. Ask Babble, he'll back me up.'

'I can't back you up,' Babble said. 'I have nothing more to go on than they do. I have only your oral statement.'

Seth Morley said, 'What was Tony using as a weapon?'

'A sword,' Belsnor said. 'You can see that; it's still there with him in his room.'

'Where did you get the gun you shot him with?' Russell said.

'I had it,' Belsnor said. He felt sick and weak. 'I did what I could,' he said. 'I did what I had to.'

'So "they" aren't responsible for all the deaths,' Seth Morley said. 'You are responsible for Tony Dunkelwold's death and he's responsible for Bert's.'

'Dunkelwelt,' Belsnor corrected, aimlessly.

'And we don't know if Mrs Rockingham is dead; she may just have roamed off. Possibly out of fear.'

'She couldn't,' Belsnor said. 'She was too ill.'

'I think,' Seth Morley said, 'that Frazer is right. We need a different leader.' To Babble he said, 'Where's his gun?'

'He left it in Tony's room,' Babble said.

Belsnor slid away from them, in the direction of Tony Dunkelwelt's living quarters.

'Stop him,' Babble said.

Ignatz Thugg, Wade Frazer, Seth Morley and Babble hurried past Belsnor; in a group they trotted up the steps and on to the porch and then into Tony's quarters. Russell stood aloof; he remained with Belsnor and Maggie Walsh.

Coming out of Tony's doorway, Seth Morley held the gun in his hand and said, 'Russell, don't you think we're doing the right thing?'

'Give him back his gun,' Russell said.

Surprised, Seth Morley halted. But he did not bring the gun over to Belsnor. 'Thanks,' Belsnor said to Russell. 'I can use the support.' To Morley and the others he said,

'Give me the gun, as Russell says. It isn't loaded anyhow; I took the shells out.' He held out his hand and waited.

Coming back down the steps from the porch, and still carrying the gun, Seth Morley said with grave reservations, 'You killed someone.'

'He had to,' Russell said.

'I'm keeping the gun,' Seth Morley said.

'My husband is going to be your leader,' Mary Morley said. 'I think it's a very good idea; I think you'll find him excellent. At Tekel Upharsin he held a position of large authority.'

'Why don't you join them?' Belsnor said to Russell.

'Because I know what happened. I know what you had to do. If I can manage to talk to them maybe I can—' He broke off. Belsnor turned toward the group of men to see what was happening.

Ignatz Thugg held the gun. He had grabbed it away from Morley; now he held it pointed at Belsnor, a seedy, twisted grin on his face.

'Give it back,' Seth Morley said to him; all of them were shouting at Thugg, but he stood unmoved, still pointing the gun at Belsnor.

'I'm your leader, now,' Thugg said. 'With or without a vote: You can vote me in if you want, but it doesn't matter.' To the three men around him he said, 'You go over there where they are. Don't get too close to me. You understand?'

'It's not loaded,' Belsnor repeated.

Seth Morley looked crushed, his face had a pale, dry cast to it, as if he knew – obviously he knew – that he had been responsible for Thugg getting possession of the gun.

Maggie Walsh said, 'I know what to do.' She reached into her pocket and brought out a copy of Specktowsky's Book.

In her mind she knew that she had found the way to get the gun away from Ignatz Thugg. Opening The Book at random she walked towards him, and as she walked she read aloud from The Book. ' "Hence it can be said," ' she intoned, ' "that God-in-history shows several phases: (one) The period of purity before the Form Destroyer was awakened into activity. (two) The period of the Curse, when the power of the Deity was weakest, the power of the Form Destroyer was greatest – this because God had not perceived the Form Destroyer and so was taken by surprise. (three) The birth of God-on-Earth, sign that the period of Absolute Curse and Estrangement from God had ended. (four) The period now—" ' She had come almost up to him; he stood unmoving, still holding the gun. She continuing to read the sacred text aloud. ' "The period now, in which God walks the world, redeeming the suffering now, redeeming all life later through the figure of himself as the Intercessor who —" '

'Go back with them,' Thugg told her. 'Or I'll kill you.'

' "Who, it is sure, is still alive, but not in this circle. (five) The next and last period—" '   .

A terrific *bang* boomed at her eardrums; deafened, she moved a step back and then felt great pain in her chest; she felt her lungs die from the great, painful shock of it. The scene around her became dull, the light faded and she saw only darkness. Seth Morley, she tried to say, but no sound came out. And yet she heard noise; she heard something huge and far off, chugging violently into the darkness.

She was alone.

Thud, thud, came the noise. Now she saw iridescent colour, mixed into a light which travelled like a liquid; it formed buzzsaws and pinwheels and crept upward on each side of her. Directly before her the huge Thing throbbed menacingly; she heard its imperative, angry voice summoning her upward. The urgency of its activity frightened her; it demanded, rather than asked. It was telling her something; she knew what it meant by its enormous pounding. Wham, wham, wham, it went and, terrified, filled with physical pain, she called to it. *Libera me,*

Domine,' she said. *'De morte aeterna, in die illa tremenda.'*

It throbbed on and on. And she glided helplessly towards it. Now, on the periphery of her vision, she saw a fantastic spectacle; she saw a great crossbow and on it the Intercessor. The string was pulled back; the Intercessor was placed on it like an arrow; and then, soundlessly, the Intercessor was shot upward, into the smallest of the concentric rings.

'Agnus Dei,' she said, *'qui tollis peccata mundi.'* She had to look away from the throbbing vortex; she looked down and back . . . and saw, far below her, a vast frozen landscape of snow and boulders. A furious wind blew across it; as she watched, more snow piled up around the rocks. A new period of glaciation, she thought, and found that she had trouble thinking – let alone talking – in English. *'Lacrymosa dies illa,'* she said, gasping with pain; her entire chest seemed to have become a block of suffering. *'Qua resurget ex favilla, judicandus homo reus.'* It seemed to make the pain less, this need to express herself in Latin – a language which he had never studied and knew nothing about. *'Huic ergo parce, Deus!'* she said. *'Pie Jesu Domine, dona eis requiem.'* The throbbing continued on.

A chasm opened before her feet. She began to fall; below her the frozen landscape of the hell-world grew closer. Again she cried out, *'Libera me, Domine, de morte aeterna!'* But she still fell; she had almost reached the hell-world, and nothing meant to lift her up.

Something with immense wings soared up, like a great metallic dragon fly with spines jutting from its head. It passed her, and a warm wind billowed after it. *'Salve me, fons pietatis,'* she called to it; she recognized it and felt no surprise at seeing it. The Intercessor, fluttering up from the hell-world, back to the fire of the smaller, inner rings.

Lights, in various colours, bloomed on all sides of her; she saw a red, smoky light burning close and, confused, turned toward it. But something made her pause. *The wrong colour,* she thought to herself. I should be looking for a clear, white light, the proper womb in which to be reborn. She drifted upward, carried by the warm wind of the Intercessor . . . the smoky red light fell behind and in its place, to her right, she saw a powerful, unflickering, yellow light. As best she could she propelled herself toward that.

The pain in her chest seemed to have lessened; in fact her entire body felt vague. Thank you, she thought, for easing the discomfort; I appreciate that. I have seen it, she said to herself; I have seen the Intercessor and through it I have a chance of surviving. Lead me, she thought. Take me to the proper colour of light. To the right new birth.

The clear, white light appeared. She yearned towards it, and something helped propel her. Are you angry at me? she thought, meaning the enormous presence that throbbed. She could still hear the throbbing, but it was no longer meant for her; it would throb on throughout eternity because it was beyond time, outside of time, never having been in time. And – there was no space present, either; everything appeared two dimensional and squeezed together, like robust but crude figures drawn by a child or by some primitive man. Bright colourful figures, but absolutely flat . . . and touching.

'Mors stupebit et natura,' she said aloud. 'Cum resurget creatura, judicanti responsura.' Again the throbbing lessened. It has forgiven me, she said to herself. It is letting the Intercessor carry me to the right light.

Toward the clear, white light she floated, still uttering from time to time pious Latin phrases. The pain in her chest had gone now entirely and she felt no weight; her body had ceased to consume both time and space.

Wheee, she thought. This is marvellous.

Throb, throb, went the Central Presence, but no longer for her; it throbbed for others, now.

The Day of the Final Audit had come for her – had come and now had passed. She had been judged and the judgement was favourable. She experienced utter, absolute joy. And continued, like a moth among novas, to flutter upwards towards the proper light.

'I didn't mean to kill her,' Ignatz Thugg said huskily. He stood gazing down at the body of Maggie Walsh. 'I didn't know what she was going to do. I mean, she kept walking and walking; I thought she was after the gun.' He jerked an accusing shoulder toward Glen Belsnor. 'And he said it was empty.'

Russell said, 'She was going for the gun; you're right.'

'Then I didn't do wrong.' Thugg said.

No one spoke for a time.

'I'm not giving up the gun,' Thugg said presently.

'That's right, Thugg,' Babble said. 'You keep hold of it. So we can see how many other innocent people you want to kill.'

'I didn't want to kill her.' Thugg pointed the gun at Dr Babble. 'I've never killed nobody before. Who wants the gun?' He looked around, wildly, at all of them. 'I did exactly what Belsnor did, no more and no less. We're the same, him and me. So I'm sure as hell not going to give *him* the gun.' Panting, his breath rasping in his windpipe, Thugg gripped the gun and stared huge-eyed around at all of them.

Belsnor walked over to Seth Morley. 'We've got to get it away from him.'

'I know,' Seth Morley said. But he could think of no way to get it. If Thugg had killed simply because someone – and a woman at that – had approached him reading from The Book, then he would shoot any and all of them at the slightest pretext.

Thugg now was blatantly and floridly psychotic. It was obvious. He had wanted to kill Maggie Walsh, and Seth Morley realized something now that he hadn't understood before. *Belsnor had killed but he had not wanted to. Thugg had killed for the pleasure of it.*

It made a difference. They were safe from Belsnor –

unless they became homicidal themselves. In that case, Belsnor would of course shoot. But if they did nothing provocative—

'Don't,' his wife Mary said in his ear.

'We have to get the gun back,' Seth Morley said. 'And it's my fault he has it; I let him get it away from me.' He held out his hand, held it in Ignatz Thugg's direction. 'Give it to me,' he said, and felt his body squinch up in fear; his body prepared itself for death.

TWELVE

'He'll kill you,' Russell said. He, too, walked towards Ignatz Thugg. Everyone else watched. 'We need to have that gun,' Russell said to Thugg. To Seth Morley he said. 'Probably he can get only one of us. I know that gun; it can't be fired rapidly. He'll be able to get off one shot and that'll be it.' He moved to the other side of Thugg, approaching at a wide angle. 'All right, Thugg,' he said, and held out his hand.

Thugg turned uncertainly towards him. Seth Morley moved rapidly forward, reaching.

'Goddam you, Morley,' Thugg said; the barrel of the gun swivelled back, but momentum carried Seth Morley forward. He collided with the skinny but muscular body of Ignatz Thugg – the man smelled of hair grease, urine and sweat.

'Get him now,' Belsnor yelled; he, too, ran at Thugg, reaching to grapple with him.

Cursing, Thugg tore away from Seth Morley. His face blank with psychopathic neutrality, his eyes glittering with cold, his mouth tormented into a squirming line, he fired.

Mary Morley shrieked.

Reaching with his left arm, Seth Morley touched his right shoulder and felt blood oozing through the fabric of his shirt. The noise of the shot had paralysed him; he sank to his knees, convulsed by the pain, realizing in a dim way that Thugg had shot him in the shoulder. I'm bleeding, he thought. Christ, he thought, I didn't get the gun from him. With effort he managed to open his eyes. He saw Thugg running; Thugg hurried away, pausing a time or two to fire. But he hit no one; they had all scattered, even Belsnor. 'Help me,' Seth Morley grated, and Belsnor and Russell and Dr Babble sneaked their way to him, their attention fixed on Thugg.

At the far end of the compound, by the entrance to the briefing room, Thugg halted; gasping for breath he aimed the gun at Seth Morley and fired one more shot. It passed Morley; it did not strike. Then, with a shudder, Thugg turned away again and jogged off, leaving them.

'Frazer!' Babble exclaimed. 'Help us get Morley into the infirmary! Come on; he's bleeding from a severed artery, I think.'

Wade Frazer hurried over. He, Belsnor and Ned Russell lifted Seth up and began the task of carrying him to the doctor's infirmary.

'You're not going to croak,' Belsnor gasped as they laid him on to the long metal-topped table. 'He got Maggie but he didn't get you.' Standing back from the table, Belsnor got out a handkerchief and, shaking as he did so, blew his nose. 'That pistol should have stayed with me. Can you see that now?'

'Shut up and get out of here,' Babble said, as he snapped on the sterilizer and rapidly placed surgical instruments in it. He then tied a tourniquet around Seth Morley's injured shoulder. The flow of blood continued; it had now formed a pool on the table beside Seth Morley. 'I'll have to open him up, get the artery ends, and fuse them together,' he said. He tossed the tourniquet away, then turned on the artificial blood-supply machinery. Using a small surgical tool to drill a hole in Seth Morley's side, he adroitly fastened the feeder-tube of the artificial blood-supply. 'I can't stop him from bleeding,' he said. 'It'll take ten minutes to dig in, get the artery ends and fuse them. But he won't bleed to death.' Opening the sterilizer, he got out a tray of steaming tools. Expertly, hastily, he began to cut away Seth Morley's clothing. A moment later and he had begun exploring the injured shoulder.

'We're going to have to keep a continual watch for Thugg,' Russell said. 'Damn it, I wish there were other weapons available. That one gun, and he's got it.'

Babble said, 'I have a tranquillizing gun.' He got out a set of keys, tossed them to Belsnor. 'That locked cabinet over there.' He pointed. 'The key with the diamond-shaped head.'

Russell unlocked the cabinet and got out a long tube with a telescopic sighting device on it. 'Well, well,' he said. 'These can be handy. But do you have any ammunition besides tranquillizers? I know the amount of tranquillizers these hold; it would stun him, maybe, but—'

'Do you want to finish him off?' Babble said, pausing in his investigation of Seth Morley's shoulder.

Presently Belsnor said, 'Yes.' Russell, too, nodded.

'I have other ammo for it,' Babble said. 'Ammo that will kill. As soon as I'm finished with Morley I'll get it.'

Lying on the table, Seth Morley managed to make out the sight of Babble's tranquillizer gun. Will that protect us? he wondered. Or will Thugg make his way back here and kill all of us or possibly just kill me as I lie here helpless. 'Belsnor,' he gasped, 'don't let Thugg come back here tonight and kill me.'

'I'll stay with you,' Belsnor said; he gave him a thump with the edge of his hand. 'And we'll be armed with this.' He held Babble's tranquillizing gun, scrutinizing it. He seemed more confident, now. So did the others.

'Did you give Morley any demerol?' Russell asked Dr Babble.

'I don't have time,' Babble said, and continued working.

'I'll give it to him,' Frazer said, 'if you'll tell me where it is and where the hypos are.'

'You aren't qualified to do that,' Babble said.

Frazer said, 'And you're not qualified to do surgery.'

'I have to,' Babble said. 'If I don't he'll die. But he can get by without an analgesic.'

Mary Morley, crouching down so that her head was close to her husband's, said, 'Can you stand the pain?'

'Yes,' Seth Morley said tightly.

The operation continued.

He lay in semi-darkness. Anyhow the bullet is out of me, he thought drowsily. And I've had demerol both intravenously and intermuscularly . . . and I feel nothing. Did he manage to stitch the artery properly? he wondered.

A complex machine monitored his internal activity: it kept note of his blood pressure, his heart rate, his temperature and his respiratory apparatus. But where's Babble? he wondered. And Belsnor, where is he?

'Belsnor!' he said as loudly as he could. 'Where are you? You said you'd be here with me all the time.'

A dark shape materialized. Belsnor, carrying the tranquillizer gun with both hands. 'I'm here. Calm down.'

'Where are the others?'

'Burying the dead,' Belsnor said. 'Tony Dunkelwelt, old Bert, Maggie Walsh . . . they're using some heavy digging equipment left over from the building of the settlement. And Tallchief. We're burying him, too. The first one to die. And Susie. Poor, dumb Susie.'

'Anyhow he didn't get me,' Seth Morley said.

'He wanted to. He did his best.'

'We shouldn't have tried to get the gun away from you,' Seth Morley said. He knew that, now. For what it was worth.'

'You should have listened to Russell,' Belsnor said. 'He knew.'

'Hindsight is cheap,' Seth Morley said. But Belsnor was patently right; Russell had tried to show them the way and they, from panic, had failed to listen. 'No sign of Mrs Rockingham?'

'None. We've searched throughout the settlement. She's gone; Thugg's gone. But we know he's alive. And armed and dangerous and psychopathically oriented.'

Seth Morley said, 'We don't know he's alive. He may have killed himself. Or what got Tallchief and Susie may have gotten him too.'

'Maybe. But we can't count on it.' Belsnor examined his wristwatch. 'I'll be outside; from there I can see the digging operation and still watch over you. I'll see you.' He thumped Morley on his left shoulder, then walked silently from the room and disappeared at once from sight.

Seth Morley wearily shut his eyes. The smell of death, he thought, is everywhere. We are inundated with it. How many people have we lost? he asked himself. Tallchief, Susie, Roberta Rockingham, Betty Jo Berm, Tony Dunkelwelt, Maggie Walsh, old Bert Kosler. Seven dead. Seven of us left. They've gotten half of us in less than twenty-four hours.

And for this, he thought, we left Tekel Upharsin. There is a macabre irony about it; we all came here because we wanted to live more fully. We wanted to be useful. Everyone in this colony had a dream. Maybe that's what was wrong with us, he thought. We have been lodged too deeply in our respective dream worlds. We don't seem able to come out of them; that's why we can't function as a group. And some of us, such as Thugg and Dunkelwelt – there are some of us who are functionally, outright insane.

A gun muzzle jutted against the side of his head. A voice said, 'Be quiet.'

A second man, wearing black leather, strode toward the

148

front of the infirmary, an erg-gun held ready. 'Belsnor is outside,' he said to the man holding the gun against Seth Morley's head. 'I'll take care of him.' Aiming his weapon he fired an arc of electricity; emerging from the anode coil of the gun it connected with Belsnor, turning him momentarily into a cathode terminal. Belsnor shivered, then slid down on to his knees. He fell over on one side and lay, the tranquillizer gun resting beside him.

'The others,' the man squatting next to Seth Morley said.

'They're burying their dead. They won't notice. Even his wife isn't here.' He came over to Seth Morley; the man beside him rose and both of them stood together for a moment, surveying Seth Morley. Both wore black leather and he wondered who or what they were.

'Morley,' the first man said, 'we're taking you out of here.'

'Why?' Morley said.

'To save your life,' the second man said. Swiftly they produced a stretcher and laid it beside Morley's bed.

THIRTEEN

Parked behind the infirmary a small squib-ship glistened moistly in the moon-laden night. The two men in black leather uniforms carried Morley in his stretcher to the hatch of the squib; there they set the stretcher down. One of them opened the hatch. They again picked up the stretcher and carried him carefully inside.

'Is Belsnor dead?' he asked.

The first man said, 'Stunned.'

'Where are we going?' Morley said.

'To a place you'd like to go to.' The second leather-clad

man seated himself at the control board; he threw several switches to 'on', adjusted dials and meters. The squib rose up and hurled itself into the nocturnal sky. 'Are you comfortable, Mr Morley? I'm sorry we had to put you on the floor, but this will not be a very long trip.'

'Can you tell me who you are?' Morley said.

'Just tell us,' the first man said, 'if you're comfortable.'

Morley said, 'I'm comfortable.' He could distinguish the viewscreen of the squib; on it, as if this were daylight, he saw trees and smaller flora: shrubs, lichens, and then a flash of illumination: a river.

And then, on the viewscreen, he saw the Building.

The squib prepared to land. On the Building's roof.

'Isn't that right?' the first man in black leather said.

'Yes.' Morley nodded.

'Do you still want to go there?'

He said, 'No.'

'You don't remember this place,' the first man said. 'Do you?'

'No,' Morley said. He lay breathing shallowly, trying to conserve his strength. 'I saw it today for the first time,' he said.

'Oh no,' the second man said. 'You've seen it before.'

Warning lights on the Building's roof glinted as the squib bounced to an unskilled landing.

'Damn that RK beam,' the first man said. 'It's erratic again. I was right; we should have come in on manual.'

'I couldn't land on this roof,' the second man said. 'It's too irregular. I'd hit one of those hydro-towers.'

'I don't think I want to work with you any more,' the first man said, 'if you can't land a size B ship on a roof this large.'

'It has nothing to do with size. What I'm complaining about is the random obstructions. There're too many of them.' He went to the hatch and manually cranked it open. Night air smelling of violets drifted in . . . and, with it, the dull, moaning roar of the Building.

Seth Morley scrambled to his feet; at the same time he strained to get his fingers on the erg-gun held loosely by the man at the hatch.

The man was slow to react; he had looked away from Seth Morley for a moment, asking the man at the control board something – in any case he did not see Seth Morley in time. His companion had already shouted a warning before he reacted.

In Seth Morley's grip the erg-gun slithered and escaped from him; he fell on it deliberately, struggling to get hold of it once again.

A high-frequency electrical impulse, released by the man at the control board shimmered past him. The man had missed. Seth Morley flopped back on to his good shoulder, dragged himself to a quasi-sitting position, and fired back.

The beam touched the man at the control board; it caught him above the right ear. At the same time, Seth Morley swivelled the gun barrel; he shot the man tumbling vainly over him. At such close range the impact of the beam was enormous; the man convulsed, fell backward, tumbled with a loud crash into a complex of instrumentation mounted against the far wall of the squib.

Morley slammed the hatch, turned it to lock, then sank down on to the floor. Blood seeped through the bandage on his shoulder, befouling the area adjacent to him. His head hummed and he knew that he would, in a moment or two, pass entirely out.

A speaker mounted above the control board clicked on. 'Mr Morley,' it said, 'we know that you have taken control of the squib. We know that both our men are unconscious. Please do not take off. Your shoulder was not operated on properly; the junction of torn pieces of artery was unsuccessful. If you do not open the hatch of the squib and let us render you major and immediate medical assistance, then you probably will not live another hour.'

The hell with you, Seth Morley thought. He crept towards the control board, reached one of its two seats; with his good arm he hoisted himself up, groped to steady himself and, gradually, pulled himself into place.

'You are not trained to pilot a high-speed squib,' the speaker said. Evidently monitors of some sort, within the squib, were telling them what he was doing.

'I can fly it,' he said, snorting for breath; his chest seemed weighted down and he had immense difficulty inhaling. On the dashboard a group of switches were marked as being tape-programmed flight patterns. Eight in all. He selected one at random, pressed the switch shut.

Nothing happened.

It's still on the incoming beam, he realized. I have to release the beam lock.

He found the lock, clicked it off. The squib shivered and then, by degrees, rose up into the night sky.

Something is wrong, he said to himself. The squib isn't handling right. The flaps must still be in the landing position.

By now he could barely see. The cab of the vehicle had begun to dim around him; he shut his eyes, shuddered, opened his eyes once more. Christ, he thought; I'm passing out. Will this thing crash without me? Or will it go somewhere, and if so, where?

He fell, then, toppling from the seat and on to the floor of the squib. Blackness collected around him and included him within itself.

As he lay on the floor unconscious the squib flew on and on.

Baleful white light dinned into his face; he felt the scorching brilliance, squeezed his eyes shut again – but he could not suppress it. 'Stop,' he said; he tried to put up his arms, but they did not move. At that, he managed to open his eyes; he gazed around, trembling with weakness.

The two men in black leather uniforms lay quietly . . . exactly as he had last seen them. He did not have to examine them to know that they were dead. *Belsnor, then, was dead*; the weapon did not stun – it killed.

Where am I now? he wondered.

The viewscreen of the squib was still on, but it's lens fed directly into an obstruction of some sort; on it he saw only a flat, white surface.

Rotating the ball which controlled the sweep of the viewscreen he said to himself, a lot of time has passed. He touched his injured shoulder cautiously. The bleeding had stopped. Perhaps they had lied to him; perhaps Babble had done an adequate job after all.

Now the viewscreen showed—

A great dead city. Under him. The squib had come to rest at a field up in the higher spires of the city's building-web.

No movement. No life. No one lived in the city; he saw in the viewscreen decay and absolute, endless collapse. As if, he thought, this is the city of the Form Destroyer.

The speaker mounted above the control board made no sound. He would get no help from *them*.

Where the hell can I be? he asked himself. Where in the galaxy is there a city of this size which has been abandoned, allowed to die? Left to erode and rot away. It has been dead for a century! he said to himself, appalled.

Rising unsteadily to his feet he crept to the hatch of the squib. Opening it electrically – he did not have enough strength to operate the quicker manual crank – he peered out.

The air smelled stale and cold. He listened. No sound.

Summoning his strength he lurched haltingly out of the squib, on to the roof top.

There is no one here, he said to himself.

Am I still on Delmak-O? he wondered.

He thought, *There is no place like this on Delmak-O.* Because Delmak-O is a new world to us; we never colonized it. Except for our one small settlement of fourteen people.

And this is old!

He clambered unstably back into the squib, stumbled to the control board and awkwardly reseated himself. There he sat for a time, meditating. What should I do? he asked himself. I've got to find my way back to Delmak-O, he decided. He examined his watch. Fifteen hours had passed – roughly – since the two men in black leather uniforms had kidnapped him. Are the others in the group still alive? he wondered. Or did they get all of them?

The automatic pilot; it had a voice-control box.

He snapped it on and said into the microphone, 'Take me to Delmak-O. At once.' He shut the microphone off, leaned back to rest himself, waited.

The ship did nothing.

'Do you know where Delmak-O is?' he said into the microphone. 'Can you take me there? You were there fifteen hours ago; you remember, don't you?' Nothing. No response, no movement. No sound of its ion-propulsion engine cackling into activity. There is no Delmak-O flight pattern engrammed into it, he realized. The two leather-clad men had taken the squib there on manual, evidently. Or else he was operating the equipment incorrectly.

Gathering his faculties, he inspected the control board. He read everything printed on its switches, dials, knobs, control-ball . . . every written declaration. No clue. He could learn nothing from it – least of all how to operate it manually. I can't go anywhere, he said to himself, because I don't know where I am. All I could do would be to fly at random. Which presupposes that I figure out how to operate this thing manually.

One switch caught his eye; he had missed it the first time around. REFERENCE, the switch read. He snapped it on. For a time nothing happened. And then the speaker above the control board squawked into life.

'Your query.'

He said, 'Can you tell me my location?'

'You want FLIGHT INFO.'

'I don't see anything on the panel marked FLIGHT INFO,' he said.

'It is not on the panel. It is mounted above the panel to your right.'

He looked. There it was.

Snapping the FLIGHT INFO unit into operating position, he said, 'Can you tell me where I am?'

Static, the semblance of something at work . . . he heard a faint zzzzzz sound: almost a whirr. A mechanical device had slid into activity. And then, from the speaker, a vodor voice, an electronic matching of human vocal sound. 'Yezzz sirrr. Euuuu arrrr in London.'

'London!' he echoed, dazed. 'How can that be?'

'Euuuu fluuuu there.'

He struggled with that but could make nothing out of it. 'You mean the city of London, England, on Terra?' he asked.

'Yezzz sirrr.'

After a time he managed to pull himself together enough to put another question to it. 'Can I fly to Delmak-O in this squib?'

'That izzz a six-year flighttt. Euuuur squib is not equipped for such a flighttt. Forrr example it doesss not possess enough thrust to breakkk euuuu freeeee from the planet.'

'Terra,' he said thickly. Well, it explained the deserted city. All the big cities on Terra were – he had heard – deserted. They no longer served any purpose. There was no population to house itself in them because everyone, except the ostriches, had emigrated.

'My squib, then,' he said, 'is a local high-velocity shuttle vessel, for homoplanetary flight only?'

'Yesss sirrr.'

'Then I could fly here to London only from another locus on the planet.'

'Yesss sirrr.'

Morley, his head ringing, his face damp with grease-like

drops of perspiration, said, 'Can you retroplot my previous course? Can you determine where I came here from?'

'Certainly.' A protracted wheeze from the mechanism. 'Yezzz. Euuuu flewww here from the following origination: #3R68-222B. And before thattt—'

'The ident notation is incomprehensible to me,' Morley said. 'Can you translate that into words?'

'Nooo. There are nooo wordzzz to describe it.'

'Can you programme my squib to returnfly there?'

'Yezzz. I can feed the coordinates into euuuur flight-control assembly. I am also equipped to accident-arrest monitor the flighttt; shall I do thattt?'

'Yes,' he said, and slumped, exhausted and pain-filled, against the horizontal frame of the control board.

The FLIGHT INFO unit said, 'Sirrr, do you need medical attentionnn?'

'Yes,' Morley said.

'Dooo you wish your squibbb to shuttle euuuu to the nearest medical station?'

He hesitated. Something at work in the deeper parts of his mind told him to say no. 'I'll be all right,' he said. 'The trip won't take long.'

'Nooo sirrr. T-ank euuuu, sirrr. I am now feeding the co-ordinates for a flight to #3R68-222B. And I will accident-arrest monitor euuuur flight; isss that correct?'

He could not answer. His shoulder had begun bleeding once more; evidently he had lost more blood than he realized.

Lights, as on a player piano, lit up before him; he vaguely made their winking warmth out. Switches opened and shut . . . it was like resting his head on a pinball machine prepared to release a free game – in this case a black and dismal free game. And then, smoothly, the squib rose up into the midday sky; it circled London – if it actually was London – and then headed west.

'Give me oral confirmation,' he grunted. 'When we get there.'

156

'Yezzz sirrr. I will awaken euuuu.'

'Am I really talking to a machine?' Morley murmured.

'Technically I am an inorganic artificial constructtt in the proto-computer classss. But—' It rambled on, but he did not hear it; once again Seth Morley had passed out.

The squib continued its short flight.

'We are approaching coordinates #3R68-222B,' a shrill voice squeaked in his ear, jarring him awake.

'Thanks,' he said, lifting his heavy head to peer cloudily into the viewscreen. A massive entity loomed up in the viewscreen; for a moment he could not identify it – most certainly it was not the settlement – *and then, with horror, he realized that the squib had returned to the Building.* 'Wait,' he said frantically. 'Don't land?'

'But we are at coordinates #3R68—'

'I countermand that order,' he snapped. 'Take me to the coordinates prior to that.'

A pause, and then the FLIGHT INFO unit said, 'The previousssss flight originated at a locussss manually plotted. Hence there isss nooo recorddd of it in the guide-assembly. There isss nooo way I can compute ittt.'

'I see,' he said. It did not really surprise him. 'Okay,' he said, watching the Building below become smaller and smaller; the squib was rising from it to flap about in a circle overhead. 'Tell me how to assume manual control of this craft.'

'Firssst euuuu push switch tennn for override cancellation. Then – doo euuuu seee that large plastic ball? Euuuu roll that from side to side and forwarddd and backkk: that controlsss the flight path of euuuur smalll craft. I suggest euuuu practise before I release controlll.'

'Just release control,' he said savagely. Far below, he saw two black dots rising from the Building.

'Control released.'

He rotated the big plastic ball. The squib at once

bucked, floundered; it shuddered and then plunged nose-first toward the dry lands below.

'Back, back,' FLIGHT INFO said warningly. 'Euuuur descending too fassst.'

He rolled the ball back and this time found himself on a reasonably horizontal course.

'I want to lose those two ships following me,' he said.

'Euuuur ability to manoeuvre thisss craft isss not such that—'

'Can you do it?' he broke in.

The FLIGHT INFO unit said, 'I possess a variety of random flight-patternss, any one of which would tend to throwww them offf.'

'Pick one,' Morley said, 'and use it.' The two pursuing ships were much closer, now. And, in the viewscreen, he saw the barrel of a cannon poking from the nose of each, a .88 millimetre barrel. Any second now they would open fire.

'Random course in operation, sirrr,' the FLIGHT INFO unit told him. 'Pleeezzz strap eurrself in, sirrr.'

He haltingly fiddled with the seat belt. As he clicked the buckle into place his squib abruptly shot upward, rolling into an immelmann loop . . . it came out of the manoeuvre flying in the opposite direction, and well above the pursuing ships.

'Radar fixxx on usss, sirrr,' the FLIGHT INFO unit informed him. 'From the aforementioned two vessels. I shall programme the flight-control assembly to take proper evasive action. Therefore we will shortly be flying close to the groundddd. Do not be alarmed.' The ship plunged down like a deranged elevator; stunned, he rested his head on his arm and shut his eyes. Then, equally abruptly, the squib levelled off. It flew erratically, compensating from moment to moment against altitude-variations in the terrain.

He lay resting in his seat, sickened by the up-and-down gyrations of the ship.

Something boomed dully. One of the pursuing ships had either fired its cannon or released an air-to-air missile. Swiftly coming awake he studied the viewscreen. Had it been close?

He saw, far off, across the wild terrain, a tall column of black smoke arising. The shot had been across his bow, as he had feared; it was now telling him that he had been caught.

'Are we armed in any manner?' he asked FLIGHT INFO.

FLIGHT INFO said, 'As per regulation we carry two 120-A type air-to-air missiles. Shall I programme the control carrier to activate themmm in relation to the craft following usss?'

'Yes,' he said. It was, in a way, a hard decision to make; he would be committing his first voluntary homicidal act in their – in any – direction. But they had started the firing; they had no hesitation about killing him. And if he did not defend himself they would.

'Missssilesss fired,' a new and different vodor voice sounded, this one from the central control panel itself. 'Doooo euuuu want a vizzzual scan of their activity?'

'Yesss, he doesss,' FLIGHT INFO ordered.

On the screen a different scene appeared; it was being transmitted, via a split screen, from *both* missiles.

The missile on the left side of the screen missed its target and passed on by, to descend, gradually, into a collision course with the ground. The second one, however, flew directly at its target. The pursuing ship wheeled, screamed directly upward . . . the missile altered target and then the viewscreen was suffused with silent, white light. The missile had detonated. One of the two pursuing ships had died.

The other one continued on, directly at him. Picking up velocity as it came. The pilot knew that he had fired all his armaments. Combatwise he was now helpless – and the remaining ship knew it.

'Do we have a cannon?' Morley asked.

FLIGHT INFO said, 'The small size of thisss ship doess not permit—'

'A simple yes or no.'

'No.'

'Anything, then?'

'No.'

Morley said, 'I want to give up. I'm injured and I'm bleeding to death as I sit here. Land this ship as soon as possible.'

'Yesss sirrr.' Now the squib dipped down; again it flew parallel to the ground, but this time braking, slowing its speed. He heard its wheel-lowering mechanism go into operation, with a shuddering bump, the squib touched down.

He moaned with pain as the squib bounced, quaked, then turned on an angle, its tyres squealing.

It came to a stop. Silence. He lay against the central control panel, listening for the other ship. He waited; he waited. No sound. Still only the empty silence.

'FLIGHT INFO,' he said aloud, raising his head in a palsied, trembling motion. 'Has it landed?'

'It continued on byyy.'

'Why'?

'I do not knowww. It continuesss to move away from usss; my scanner can barely pick it up.' A pause. 'Now it's beyond scanner-probe range.'

Maybe it had failed to perceive his landing. Maybe it – the pilot – had assumed his low-level, horizontal flight to be a further attempt to defeat the computerized radar.

Morley said, 'Take off again. Fly in widening circles. I'm looking for a settlement that's in this area.' He chose a course at random. 'Fly slightly northeast.'

'Yesss sirrr.' The squib pulsed with new activity and then, in a professional, competent way, rose up into the sky.

Again he rested, but this time lying so that he could perpetually scan the viewscreen. He did not really think that they would be successful; the settlement was small and the funky landscape was enormous. But – what was the alternative?

To go back to the Building. And now he had a firm, physical revulsion towards it; his earlier desire to enter it had evaporated.

It is not a winery, he said to himself. But what the hell is it, then?

He did not know. And he hoped he never would.

Something glinted to the right. Something metallic. He roused himself groggily. Looking at the control board clock he saw that squib had been flying in widening circles for almost an hour. Did I drift off? he wondered. Squinting, he peeped to see what had glinted. Small buildings.

He said, 'That's it.'

'Shall I land there?'

'Yes.' He hunched forward, straining to see. Straining to be sure.

It was the settlement.

FOURTEEN

A small – heartbreakingly small – group of men and women trudged wanly up to the parked squib as Seth Morley activated the electrical dehatching mechanism. They stared at him bleakly as he stumbled out, stood swaying, trying to get control of his waning vitality.

There they were. Russell, looking stern. His wife Mary, her face taut with alarm – then relief at seeing him. Wade Frazer, who looked tired. Dr Milton Babble, chewing on his pipe in a reflexive, pointless way. Ignatz Thugg was not among them.

Neither was Glen Belsnor.

Leadenly, Seth Morley said, 'Belsnor is dead, isn't he?'
They nodded.

Russell said, 'You're the first of all of them to come
back. We noticed late last night that Belsnor wasn't guard-
ing us. We got to him at the infirmary door; he was already
dead.'

'Electrocuted,' Dr Babble said.

'And you were gone,' Mary said. Her eyes remained
glazed and hopeless, despite his return.

'You better get back into bed in the infirmary,' Babble
said to him. 'I don't know how you could still be alive.
Look at you; you're drenched with blood.'

Together, they assisted him back to the infirmary. Mary
fussily made up the bed; Seth Morley, swaying, stood waiting and then let them stretch his body out, propped up by
pillows.

'I'm going to work on your shoulder some more,' Babble
said to him. 'I think the artery is allowing seepage out into
the—'

Seth Morley said, 'We're on Earth.'

They stared at him. Babble froze; he turned towards Seth,
then mechanically returned to his task of fumbling with a
tray of surgical instruments. Time passed, but no one
spoke.

'What is the Building?' Wade Frazer said, at last.

'I don't know. But they say I was there, once.' So on
some level I do know, he realized. Maybe we all do. Perhaps at some time in the past all of us were there.
Together.

'Why are they killing us?' Babble said.

'I don't know that either,' Seth Morley answered.

Mary said, 'How do you know we're on Earth?'

'I was at London a little while ago. I saw it, the ancient,
abandoned city. Mile after mile of it. Thousands of decaying, deserted houses, factories and streets. Bigger than any

162

non-terran city anywhere in the galaxy. Where at one time six million people lived.'

Wade Frazer said, 'But there's nothing on Terra except the aviary! And nobody except ostriches!'

'Plus Interplan West military barracks and research installations,' Seth Morley said, but his voice ebbed; it lacked conviction and enthusiasm. 'We're an experiment,' he said, anyhow. 'As we guessed last night. A military experiment being carried out by General Treaton.' But he did not believe it either. 'What kind of military personnel wear black leather uniforms?' he said. 'And jackboots . . . I think they're called.'

Russell, in a modulated, disinterested voice, said, 'Aviary guards. A sop to keep up their morale. It's very discouraging to work around ostriches; introduction of the new uniforms, three or four years back, has done a great deal of morale-boosting for the personnel.'

Turning towards him, Mary said searchingly, 'How do you happen to know that?'

'Because,' Russell said, still calm, 'I am one of them.' Reaching into his jacket he brought out a small, shiny erg-gun. 'We carry this type of weapon.' He held the gun pointed toward them, meanwhile motioning them to stand closer together. 'It was one chance out of a million that Morley got away.' Russell pointed to his right ear. 'They've been periodically keeping me informed. I knew he was on his way back here, but I – and my various superiors – never thought he'd arrive.' He smiled at them. Graciously.

A sharp *thump* sounded. Loudly.

Russell half-turned, lowered his erg-gun and slumped down, letting the weapon fall. What is it? Seth Morley asked himself; he sat up, trying to see. He made out a shape, the shape of a man, walking into the room. The Walker? he thought. The Walker-on-Earth come to save us? The man held a gun – an old-fashioned lead slug pistol. Belsnor's gun, he realized. But Ignatz Thugg has it. He did not understand. Neither did the others; they milled about incoherently as the man, holding the pistol, walked up to them.

It was Ignatz Thugg.

On the floor, Russell lay dying. Thugg bent, picked up the erg-gun, and put it away in his belt.

'I came back,' Thugg said grimly.

'Did you hear him?' Seth Morley said. 'Did you hear Russell say that—'

Thugg said, 'I heard him.' He hesitated, then brought out the erg-gun; he handed it to Morley. 'Somebody get the tranquillizer gun,' he said. 'We'll need all three. Are there any more? In the squib?'

'Two in the squib,' Seth Morley said, accepting the erg-gun from Thugg. You're not going to kill us? he wondered. The psychopathic countenance of Ignatz Thugg had relaxed; the strained attentiveness which had marked Thugg had relented. Thugg looked calm and alert; sanely so.

'You're not my enemies,' Thugg said. 'They are.' He gestured with Belsnor's pistol toward Russell. 'I knew someone in the group was; I thought it was Belsnor, but I was wrong. I'm sorry.' He was silent for a time.

The rest of them remained silent, too. Waiting to see what would happen. It would come soon, they all knew. Five weapons, Seth Morley said to himself. Pitiful. They have air-to-ground missiles, .88 millimetre cannon – God knows what else. Is it worth it, trying to fight them?

'It is,' Thugg said, evidently reading his expression.

Seth Morley said, 'I think you're right.'

'I think I know,' Wade Frazer said, 'what this experiment is all about.' The others waited for him to go on but he did not.

'Say it,' Babble said.

'Not until I'm sure,' Frazer said.

Seth Morley thought, I think I know, too. And Frazer is

164

right; until we know absolutely, until we have total proof, we had better not even discuss it.

'I knew we were on Terra,' Mary Morley said quietly. 'I recognized the moon; I've seen Luna in pictures . . . a long time ago when I was a child.'

'And what did you infer from that?' Wade Frazer said.

Mary said, 'I—' She hesitated, glancing at her husband. 'Isn't it a military experiment by Interplan West? As all of us suspected?'

'Yes,' Seth Morley said.

'There's another possibility,' Wade Frazer said.

'Don't say it,' Seth Morley said.

'I think we had better say it,' Wade Frazer said. 'We should face it openly, decide if it's true, and then decide whether we want to go on and fight them.'

'Say it,' Babble said, stammering from over-intensity.

Wade Frazer said, 'We're criminally insane. And at one time, probably for a long time, maybe years, we were kept inside what we call "the Building".' He paused. The Building, then, would be both a prison and a mental hospital. A prison for the—'

'What about our settlement?' Babble said.

'An experiment,' Frazer said. 'But not by the military. By the prison and hospital authorities. To see if we could function on the outside . . . on a planet supposedly far away from Terra. And we failed. We began to kill one another.' He pointed at the tranquillizing gun. 'That's what killed Tallchief; that's what started it all off. You did it, Babble. You killed Tallchief. Did you also kill Susie Smart?'

'I did not,' Babble said thinly.

'But you did kill Tallchief.'

'Why?' Ignatz Thugg asked him.

Babble said, 'I – guessed what we were. I thought Tallchief was what Russell turned out to be.'

'Who killed Susie Smart?' Seth Morley asked Frazer.

'I don't know. I have no clue to that. Maybe Babble.

Maybe you, Morley. Did you do it?' Frazer eyed Seth Morley. 'No, I guess you didn't. Well, maybe Ignatz did it. But my point is made; any one of us could have done it. We all have the inclination. *That's what got us into the Building.'*

Mary said, 'I killed Susie.'

'Why?' Seth Morley said. He could not believe it.

'Because of what she was doing with you.' His wife's voice was ultra calm. 'And she tried to kill me; she had that replica of the Building trained. I did it in self-defence; she engineered it all.'

'Christ,' Seth Morley said.

'Did you love her that much?' Mary demanded. 'That you can't understand why I would do it?'

Seth Morley said, 'I barely knew her.'

'You knew her well enough to—'

'Okay,' Ignatz Thugg broke in. 'It doesn't matter, now. Frazer made his point; we all might have done it, and in every case one of us did.' His face twitched spasmodically. 'I think you're wrong. I just don't believe it. We can't be criminally insane.'

'The killings,' Wade Frazer said. 'I've known for a long time that everyone here was potentially homicidal. There's a great deal of autism, of schizophrenic lack of adequate affect.' He indicated Mary Morley scathingly. 'Look how she tells about murdering Susie Smart. As if it's nothing at all.' He pointed at Dr Babble. 'And his account of Tallchief's death – Babble killed a man he didn't even know . . . just in case – in case! – he might be some kind of authority figure. *Any* kind of authority figure.'

After an interval Dr Babble said, 'What I can't fathom is, Who killed Mrs Rockingham? That fine, dignified, educated woman . . . she never did any harm.'

'Maybe nobody did kill her,' Seth Morley said. 'She was infirm; maybe they came for her, the way they came for me. To remove her so she'd survive. That's the reason they gave me for coming after me and taking me away; they said

Babble's work on my shoulder was defective and I would soon die.'

'Do you believe that?' Ignatz Thugg asked.

Truthfully, Seth Morley said, 'I don't know. It might have been. After all, they could have shot me here, the way they did Belsnor.' He thought, Is Belsnor the only one they killed? And we did the rest? It supported Frazer's theory . . . and they might not have intended to kill Belsnor; they were in a hurry and evidently they thought their erg-guns were set on stun.

And they were probably afraid of us.

'I think,' Mary said, 'that they interfered with us as little as possible. After all, this was an experiment; they wanted to see how it would come out. And then they did see how it was coming out, so they sent Russell here . . . and they killed Belsnor. But maybe they saw nothing wrong with killing Belsnor; he had killed Tony. Even we understand the—' She searched for the word.

'Unbalance,' Frazer said.

'Yes, the unbalanced quality in that. He could have gotten the sword some other way.' Lightly, she put her hand on her husband's injured shoulder. Very lightly, but with feeling. 'That's why they wanted to save Seth. *He hadn't killed anyone;* he was innocent. And you—' She snarled at Ignatz Thugg, snarled with hatred. 'You would have slipped in and murdered him as he lay here hurt.'

Ignatz Thugg made a noncommittal gesture. Of dismissal.

'And Mrs Rockingham,' Mary finished. 'She hadn't killed anybody either. So they saved her, too. In the breakdown of an experiment of this type it would be natural for them to try to save as—'

'All you've said,' Frazer interrupted, 'tends to indicate that I'm right.' He smiled disdainfully, as if he were personally unconcerned. As if he were not involved.

'There has to be something else at work,' Seth Morley said. 'They wouldn't have let the killings go on as long as they did. They must have known. At least until they sent Russell. But I guess by then they knew.'

'They may not be monitoring us properly,' Babble said. 'If they relied on those little artificial insects that scurry around carrying miniature TV cameras—'

'I'm sure they have more,' Seth Morley said. To his wife he said, 'Go through Russell's pockets; see what you can find. Labels in his clothing, what kind of watch or quasi-watch he's wearing, bits of paper stuck away here and there.'

'Yes,' she said, and gingerly, began to remove Russell's spick-and-span jacket.

'His wallet,' Babble said, as Mary lifted it out. 'Let me see what's in it.' He took it from her, opened it. 'Identification. Ned W. Russell, residing at the dome-colony on Sirius 3. Twenty-nine years old. Hair: brown. Eyes: brown. Height: five eleven-and-a-half. Authorized to pilot class B and C vessels.' He looked deeper into the wallet. 'Married. Here's a 3-D photo of a young woman, undoubtedly his wife.' He rummaged further. 'And this. Pictures of a baby.'

No one said anything for a time.

'Anyhow,' Babble said presently, 'there's nothing of value on him. Nothing that tells us anything.' He rolled up Russell's left sleeve. 'His watch: Omega self-winding. A good watch.' He rolled up the brown canvas sleeve a little farther. 'A tattoo,' he said. 'On the inside of his lower arm. How strange; it's the same thing I have tattooed on my arm, and in the same place.' He traced the tattoo on Russell's arm with his finger. ' "Persus 9," ' he murmured. He unfastened his cuff and rolled back his own left sleeve. There, sure enough, was the same tattoo on his arm and in exactly the same place.

Seth Morley said, 'I have one on my instep.' Strange, he thought. And I haven't thought about that tattoo in years.

'How did you get yours?' Dr Babble asked him. 'I don't remember getting mine; it's been too long. And I don't remember what it means . . . if I ever knew. It looks like some kind of identifying military service mark. A location. A military outpost at Persus 9.'

Seth looked around at the rest of the group. All of them had acutely uncomfortable – and anxious – expressions on their faces.

'All of you have the mark on you, too,' Babble said to them, after a long, long time had passed.

'Does any one of you remember when you got this mark?' Seth Morley said. 'Or why? Or what it means?'

'I've had mine since I was a baby,' Wade Frazer said.

'You were never a baby,' Seth Morley said to him.

'What an odd thing to say,' Mary said.

'I mean,' Seth Morley said, 'that it isn't possible to imagine him as a baby.'

'But that's not what you said,' Mary said.

'What difference does it make what I said?' He felt violently irritable. 'So we do have one common element – this annotation chiselled into our flesh. Probably those who are dead have it, too. Susie and the rest of them. Well, let's face it; we all have a slot of amnesia dug somewhere in our brains. Otherwise we'd know why we got this tattoo and what it means. We'd know what Persus 9 is – or was at the time the tattoo was made. I'm afraid this confirms the criminally insane theory; we were probably given these marks when we were prisoners in the Building. We don't remember that, so we don't remember this tattoo either.' He lapsed into brooding introversion, ignoring, for the time, the rest of the group. 'Like Dachau,' he said. 'I think,' he said, 'that it's very important to find out what these marks mean. It's the first really solid indication we've found as to who we are and what this settlement is. Can any of you suggest how we find out what Persus 9 means?'

'Maybe the reference library on the squib,' Thugg said.

Seth Morley said, 'Maybe. We can try that. But first I suggest we ask the tench. And I want to be there. Can you get me into the squib along with you?' Because, he said to himself, if you leave me here I will, like Belsnor, be murdered.

Dr Babble said, 'I'll see that you're gotten aboard – with this one proviso. First we ask the squib's reference libraries. If it has nothing, then we'll go searching out the tench. But if we can get it from the squib then we won't be taking such a great—'

'Fine,' Morley said. But he knew that the ship's reference service would be unable to tell them anything.

Under Ignatz Thugg's direction they began the task of getting Seth Morley – and themselves – into the small squib.

Propped up at the controls of the squib once more, Seth Morley snapped on REFERENCE. 'Yezzz sirr,' it squeaked.

'What is referred to by the designate Persus 9?' he asked.

A whirr and then it spoke in its vodor voice. 'I have no information on a Persussss 9,' REFERENCE said.

'If it were a planet, would you have a record of it?'

'Yezzz, if known to Interplan West or Interplan East authorities.'

'Thanks.' Seth Morley shut off the REFERENCE service. 'I had a feeling it wouldn't know. And I have an even stronger feeling that the tench does know.' That, in fact, the tench's ultimate purpose would be served by asking it this question.

Why he thought that he did not know.

'I'll pilot the ship,' Thugg said. 'You're too injured; you lie down.'

'There's no place to lie down because of all these people,' Seth Morley said.

They made room. And he stretched himself out gratefully. The squib, in the hands of Ignatz Thugg, zipped up into the sky. A murderer for a pilot, Seth Morley reflected. And a doctor who's a murderer.

And my wife. A murderess. He shut his eyes.

The squib zoomed on, in search of the tench.

'There it is,' Wade Frazer said, studying the viewscreen. 'Bring the ship down.'

'Okay,' Thugg said cheerfully. He moved the control ball; the ship at once began to descend.

'Will they pick up our presence?' Babble said nervously. 'At the Building?'

'Probably,' Thugg said.

'We can't turn back now,' Seth Morley said.

'Sure we can,' Thugg said. 'But nobody said anything about it.' He adjusted the controls; the ship glided to a long, smooth landing and came to rest, bumping noisily.

'Get me out,' Morley said, standing hesitantly; again his head rang. As if, he thought, a sixty cycle hum is being conducted through my brain. Fear, he thought; it's fear that's making me this way. Not my wound.

They gingerly stepped from the squib on to parched and highly arid land. A thin smell, again like something burning, reached their noses. Mary turned away from the smell, paused to blow her nose.

'Where's the river?' Seth Morley said, looking around.

The river had vanished.

Or maybe we're somewhere else, Seth Morley thought. Maybe the tench moved. And then he saw it – not far away. It had managed to blend itself almost perfectly with its local environment. Like a desert toad, he thought. Screwing itself backward into the sand.

Rapidly, on a small piece of paper, Babble wrote. He handed it, when finished, to Seth Morley. For confirmation.

WHAT IS PERSUS 9?

'That'll do.' Seth Morley handed the slip around; all of them soberly nodded. 'Okay,' he said, as briskly as he could manage. 'Put it in front of the tench.' The great globular mass of protoplasmic slush undulated slightly, as if aware of him. Then, as the question was placed before it, the tench began to shudder . . . as if, Morley thought, to get away from us. It swayed back and forth, evidently in distress. Part of it began to liquify.

Something's wrong, Seth Morley realized. It did not act like this before.

'Stand back!' Babble said warningly; he took hold of Seth Morley by his good shoulder and propelled him bodily away.

'My God,' Mary said, 'it's coming apart.' Turning swiftly, she ran; she hurried away from the tench and climbed back into the squib.

'She's right,' Wade Frazer said. He, too, retreated.

Babble said, 'I think it's going to—' A loud whine from the tench sounded, shutting out his voice. The tench swayed, changed colour; liquid oozed out from beneath it and formed a grey, disturbed pool on all sides of it. And then, as they stared fixedly in dismay, the tench ruptured. It split into two pieces, and, a moment later, into four: it had split again.

'Maybe it's giving birth,' Seth Morley said, above the eerie whine. By degrees, the whine had become more and more intense. And more and more urgent.

'It's not giving birth to anything,' Seth Morley said. 'It's breaking apart. We've killed it with our question; it isn't able to answer. And instead it's being destroyed. Forever.'

'I'll retrieve the question.' Babble knelt, whisked the slip of paper back from its spot close to the tench.

The tench exploded.

They stood for a time, not speaking, gazing at the ruin that had been the tench. Gelatin everywhere . . . a circle of it, on all sides of the central remains. Seth Morley took a few steps forward, in its direction; Mary and the others who had run away came slipping cautiously back, to stand with him and review it. View what they had done.

'Why?' Mary demanded in agitation. 'What could there have been about a question like that—'

'It's a computer,' Seth Morley said. He could distinguish electronic components under the gelatin, exposed by the tench's explosion, the hidden core – and electronic computer – lay visible. Wiring, transistors, printed circuits, tape storage drums. Thurston gate-response crystals, basic irmadium valves by the thousand, lying scattered everywhere on the ground like minute Chinese firecrackers . . . lady crackers, they're called, Seth Morley said to himself. Pieces of it flung in all directions. Not enough left to repair; the tench, as he had intuited, was gone for good.

'So all the time it was inorganic,' Babble said, apparently dazed. 'You didn't know that, did you Morley?'

'I had an intuition,' Seth Morley said, 'but it was the wrong one. I thought it would answer – be the only living thing that could answer – the question.' How wrong he had been.

Wade Frazer said, 'You were right about one thing, Morley. That question is the key question, evidently. But where do we go from here?'

The ground surrounding the tench smoked, now, as if the gelatinous material and computer parts were starting into some kind of thermal chain reaction. The smoke had an ominous quality about it. Seth Morley, for reasons not understood, felt, sensed, the seriousness of their situation. Yes, he thought; a chain reaction which we have started but which we can't stop. How far will it go? he wondered sombrely. Already, large cracks had begun to appear in the ground adjacent to the tench. The liquid squirted from the dying, agonized tench, spilling now into the cracks . . . he heard, from far down, a low drumming noise, as if something immense and sickly-vile had been disturbed by the surface explosion.

The sky turned dark.

Incredulous, Wade Frazer said, 'Good God, Morley; what have you done with your – question?' He gestured in a seizure of motor-spasms. 'This place is breaking up!'

The man was correct. Fissions had appeared everywhere now; in a few moments there would be no safe spot to stand on. *The squib,* Seth Morley realized. We've got to get back to it. 'Babble,' he said hoarsely, 'get us all into the squib.' But Babble had gone. Looking around in the turbulent gloom, Seth Morley saw no sign of him – nor of the others.

They're in the squib already, he told himself. As best he could he made his way in that direction. Even Mary, he realized. The bastards. He falteringly reached the hatch of the squib; it hung open.

A fast-widening crack in the ground, almost six feet wide, appeared crashingly beside him; it burgeoned as he stood there. Now he found himself looking into the orifice. At the bottom something undulated. A slimy thing, very large, without eyes; it swam in a dark, stinking liquid and ignored him.

'Babble,' he croaked, and managed to make the first step that led up into the squib. Now he could see in; he clambered clumsily up, using only his good arm.

No one was in the squib.

I'm Christ-awful alone, he said to himself. Now the squib shuddered and bucked as the ground beneath it heaved. Rain had begun; he felt hot, dark drops on him, acrid rain, as if it was not water but some other less-pleasant substance. The drops seared his skin; he scrambled into the squib, stood wheezing and choking, wondering frantically where the others had gone. No sign of them. He hobbled to the squib's viewscreen . . . the squib heaved; its hull shuddered and became unstable. It's being pulled under, he said to himself. I've got to take off; I can't spend any more time searching for them. He jabbed at a button and turned on the squib's engine. Tugging on the control ball he sent the squib – with himself inside, alone – up into the dark and ugly sky . . . a sky obviously ominous to all life. He could hear the rain beating against the

174

hull; the rain of what? he wondered. Like an acid. Maybe, he thought, it will eat its way through the hull and destroy both the squib and me.

Seating himself, he clicked on the viewscreen to greatest magnification; he rotated it, simultaneously sending the squib into a rotating orbit.

On the viewscreen appeared the Building. The river, swollen and mud-coloured, angrily lapped at it. The Building, faced with its last danger, had thrown a temporary bridge across the river and, Seth Morley saw, men and women were crossing the bridge, crossing thereby the river, and going on into the Building.

They were all old. Grey and fragile, like wounded mice, they huddled together and advanced step by step in the direction of the Building. They're not going to make it, he realized. Who are they?

Peering into the viewscreen he recognized his wife. But old, like the others. Hunched over, tottering, afraid . . . and then he made out Susie Smart. And Dr Babble. Now he could distinguish them all. Russell, Ben Tallchief, Glen Belsnor, Wade Frazer, Betty Jo Berm, Tony Dunkelwelt, Babble, Ignatz Thugg, Maggie Walsh, old Bert Kosler – he had not changed, he had already been old – and Roberta Rockingham, and, at the end, Mary.

The Form Destroyer had seized them, Seth Morley realized. And done this to them. And now they are on their way back to where they came from. Forever. To die there.

The squib, around him, vibrated. Its hull clanged, again and again. Something hard and metallic was pinging off the hull. He sent the squib higher and the noise abated. What had done it? he wondered, again inspecting the viewscreen.

And then he saw.

The Building had begun to disintegrate. Parts of it, chunks of plastic and alloy bonded together, hurled as if in a giant wind up into the sky. The delicate bridge across the river broke, and as it fell it carried those crossing it to their death; they fell with the fragments of the bridge into the snarling, muddy water and vanished. But it made no difference; the Building was dying, too. They would not have been safe in it anyhow.

I'm the only one who survived, he said to himself. Moaning with grief he revolved the control ball and the ship putt-putted out of its orbit and on a tangent leading back to the settlement.

The engine of the squib died into silence.

He heard nothing, now, but the slap-slap of rain against its hull. The squib sailed in a great arc, dropping lower each moment.

He shut his eyes. I did what I could throughout, he said to himself. There was nothing more possible for me. I tried.

The squib hit, bounced, threw him from his chair on to the floor. Sections of the hull broke off, ripped away; he felt the acrid, acid-like rain pour in on him, drenching him. Opening his pain-glazed eyes he saw that the downpour had burned holes in his clothing; it was devouring his body. He perceived that in a fragment of a second – time seemed to have stopped as the squib rolled over and over, skated on its top across the terrain . . . he felt nothing, no fear, no grief, no pain any longer; he merely experienced the death of his ship – and of himself – as a kind of detached observer.

The ship skidded, at last, to a halt. Silence, except for the drip-drip of the rain of acid on him. He lay half-buried in collapsed junk: portions of the control board and viewscreen, all shattered. Jesus, he thought. Nothing is left, and presently the earth will swallow the squib and me. But it does not matter, he thought, because I am dying. In emptiness, meaninglessness and solitude. Like all the others who have gone before this fragment of the one-time group. Intercessor, he thought, intercede for me. Replace me; die for me.

He waited. And heard only the tap-tap of the rain.

FIFTEEN

Glen Belsnor removed the polyencephalic cylinder from his aching head, set it carefully down, rose unsteadily to a standing position. He rubbed his forehead and experienced pain. That was a bad one, he said to himself. We did not do well this time at all.

Going unsteadily to the dining hall of the ship he poured himself a glass of tepid, bottled water. He then rummaged in his pockets until he found his powerful analgesic tablet, popped it into his mouth, swallowed it with more of the reprocessed water.

Now, in their cubicles, the others stirred. Wade Frazer tugged at the cylinder which enclosed his brain and skull and scalp and, a few cubicles off, Sue Smart, too, appeared to be returning to active awareness of a homoencephalic kind.

As he helped Sue Smart off with her heavy cylinder he heard a groan. A lament, telling of deep suffering. It was Seth Morley, he discovered. 'Okay,' Belsnor said. 'I'll get to you as soon as I can.'

All of them were coming out of it now. Ignatz Thugg yanked violently at his cylinder, managed to detach it from its screw-lock base at his chin . . . he sat, his eyes swollen, an expression of displeasure and hostility on his wan, narrow face.

'Give me a hand,' Belsnor said. 'I think Morley is in shock. Maybe you better get Dr Babble up.'

'Morley'll be all right,' Thugg said huskily; he rubbed his eyes, grimacing as if nauseated. 'He always is.'

'But he's in shock – his death must have been a bad one.'

Thugg stood up, nodding dully. 'Whatever you say, Captain.'

'Get them warm,' Belsnor said. 'Set up the standby heat to a higher notch.' He bent over the prone Dr Milton Babble. 'Come on, Milt,' he said emphatically as he removed Babble's cylinder.

Here and there others of the crew sat up. Groaned.

Loudly, to them all, Captain Belsnor said, 'You are all right now. This one turned out to be a fiasco, but you are going – as always – to be fine. Despite what you've gone through. Dr Babble will give you a shot of something to ease the transition from polyencephalic fusion to normal homoencephalic functioning.' He waited a moment, then repeated what he had said.

Seth Morley, tremblingly, said, 'Are we aboard Persus 9?'

'You are back on the ship,' Belsnor informed him. 'Back aboard Persus 9. Do you remember how you died, Morley?'

'Something awful happened to me,' Seth Morley managed to say.

'Well,' Belsnor pointed out, 'you had that shoulder wound.'

'I mean later. After the tench. I remember flying a squib . . . it lost power and split up – disintegrated in the atmosphere. I was either torn or knocked into pieces; I was all over the squib, by the time it had finished ploughing up the landscape.'

Belsnor said, 'Don't expect me to feel sorry for you.' After all, he himself, in the polyencephalic fusion, had been electrocuted.

Sue Smart, her long hair tangled, her right breast peeping slyly from between the buttons of her blouse, gingerly touched the back of her head and winced.

'They got you with a rock,' Belsnor told her.

'But why?' Sue asked. She seemed dazed, still. 'What did I do wrong?'

Belsnor said, 'It wasn't your fault. This one turned out

178

to be a hostile one; we were venting our long-term, pent-up aggressiveness. Evidently.' He could remember, but only with effort, how he had shot Tony Dunkelwelt, the youngest member of the crew. I hope he won't be too angry, Captain Belsnor said to himself. He shouldn't be. After all, in venting his own hostility, Dunkelwelt had killed Bert Kosler, the cook of the Persus 9.

We sniffed ourselves virtually out of existence, Captain Belsnor noted to himself. I hope – I pray! – the next one is different. It should be; as in previous times we probably managed to ge rid of the bulk of our hostilities in that one fusion, that (what was it?) Delmak-O episode.

To Babble, who stood unsteadily fooling with his disarranged clothing, Belsnor said, 'Get moving, doctor. See who needs what. Pain-killers, tranquillizers, stimulants . . . they need you. But—' He leaned close to Babble. 'Don't give them anything we're low on, as I told you before, and as you ignore.'

Leaning over Betty Jo Berm, Babble said, 'Do you need some chemical-therapy help, Miss Berm?'

'I – I think I'll be okay,' Betty Jo Berm said as she sat painstakingly up. 'If I can just sit here and rest . . .' She managed a brief, cheerless smile. 'I drowned,' she said. 'Ugh.' She made a weary, but now somewhat relieved, face.

Speaking to all of them, Belsnor said quietly but with firm insistence, 'I'm reluctantly writing off that particular construct as too unpleasant to try for again.'

'But,' Frazer pointed out, lighting his pipe with shaking fingers, 'it's highly therapeutic. From a psychiatric standpoint.'

'It got out of hand,' Sue Smart said.

'It was supposed to,' Babble said as he worked with the others, rousing them, finding out what they wanted. 'It was what we call a total catharsis. Now we'll have less free-floating hostility surging back and forth between everyone here on the ship.'

Ben Tallchief said, 'Babble, I hope your hostility towards me is over.' He added, 'And for what you did to me—' He glared.

' "The ship," ' Seth Morley murmured.

'Yes,' Captain Belsnor said, slightly sardonically, amused. 'And what else have you forgotten this time? Do you want to be briefed?' He waited, but Seth Morley said nothing. Morley seemed still to be entranced. 'Give him some kind of amphetamine,' Belsnor said to Dr Babble. 'To get him into a lucid state.' It usually came to this with Seth Morley; his ability to adapt to the abrupt transition between the ship and the polyencephalically-determined worlds was negligible.

'I'll be okay,' Seth Morley said. And shut his weary eyes.

Clambering to her feet, Mary Morley came over to him, sank down beside him and put her lean hand on his shoulder. He started to slide away from her, remembering the injury to his shoulder . . . and then he discovered that, strangely, the pain had gone. Cautiously, he patted his shoulder. No injury. No blood-seeping wound. Weird, he thought. But – I guess it's always this way. As I seem to recall.

'Can I get you anything?' his wife asked him.

'Are you okay?' he asked her. She nodded. 'Why did you kill Sue Smart?' he said. 'Never mind,' he said, seeing the strong, wild expression on her face. 'I don't know why,' he said, 'but this one really bothered me. All the killing. We've never had so much of it before; it was dreadful. We should have been yanked out of this one by the psycho-circuitbreaker as soon as the first murder took place.'

'You heard what Frazer said,' Mary said. 'It was necessary; we were building too many tensions here on the ship.'

Morley thought, I see now why the tench exploded. When we asked it, What does Persus 9 mean? No wonder it blew up . . . and, with it, took the entire construct. Piece by piece.

The large, far-too-familiar cabin of the ship forced itself on to his attention. He felt a kind of dismal horror, seeing it again. To him the reality of the ship was far more unpleasant than – what had it been called? – Delmak-O, he recalled. That's right. We arranged random letters, provided us by the ship's computer ... we made it up and then we were stuck with what we made up. An exciting adventure turned into gross murder. Of all of us, by the time it had finished.

He examined his calendar wristwatch. Twelve days had passed. In real time, twelve whole, overly long days; in polyencephalic time, only a little over twenty-four hours. Unless he counted the 'eight years' at Tekel Upharsin, which he could not really do: it had been a manufactured recall-datum, implanted in his mind during fusion, to add the semblance of authenticity in the polyencephalic venture.

What did we make up? he asked himself blearily. The entire theology, he realized. They had fed into the ship's computer all the data they had in their possession concerning advanced religions. Into TENCH 889B had gone elaborated information dealing with Judaism, Christianity, Mohammedanism, Zoroastrianism, Tibetan Buddhism ... a complex mass, out of which TENCH 889B was to distill a composite religion, a synthesis of every factor involved. *We made it up,* Seth Morley thought, bewildered; memory of Specktowsky's Book still filled his mind. The Intercessor, the Mentufacturer, the Walker-on-Earth – even the ferocity of the Form Destroyer. Distillate of man's total experience with God – a tremendous logical system, a comforting web deduced by the computer from the postulates given it – in particular the postulate that God existed.

And Specktowsky ... he shut his eyes, remembering.

Egon Specktowsky had been the original captain of the ship. He had died during the accident which had disabled them. A nice touch by TENCH 889B, to make their dear former captain the author of the galaxy-wide worship which had acted as the base of this, their latest world. The awe and near-worship which they all felt for Egon Specktowsky had been neatly carried over to their episode on Delmak-O because for them, in a sense, he was a god – functioned, in their lives, as a god would. This touch had given the created world a more plausible air; it fitted in perfectly with their preconceptions.

The polyencephalic mind, he thought. Originally an escape toy to amuse us during our twenty-year voyage. But the voyage had not lasted twenty years; it would continue until they died, one by one, in some indefinably remote epoch, which none of them could imagine. And for good reason : everything, especially the infinitude of the voyage, had become an endless nightmare to them.

We could have survived the twenty years, Seth Morley said to himself. *Knowing it would end;* that would have kept us sane and alive. But the accident had come and now they circled, forever, a dead star. Their transmitter, because of the accident, functioned no longer, and so an escape toy, typical of those generally used in long, interstellar flights, had become the support for their sanity.

That's what really worries us, Morely realized. The dread that one by one we will slip into psychosis, leaving the others even more alone. More isolated from man and everything associated with man.

God, he thought, how I wish we could go back to Alpha Centaurus. If only—

But there was no use thinking about that.

Ben Tallchief, the ship's maintenance man, said, 'I can't believe that we made up Specktowsky's theology by ourselves. It seemed so real. So – airtight.'

Belsnor said, 'The computer did most of it; of course it's airtight.'

'But the basic idea was ours,' Tony Dunkelwelt said. He had fixed his attention on Captain Belsnor. 'You killed me in that one,' he said.

'We hate one another,' Belsnor said. 'I hate you; you hate me. Or at least we did before the Delmak-O episode.' Turning to Wade Frazer he said, 'Maybe you're right; I don't feel so irritated now.' Gloomily, he said, 'But it'll come back, give or take a week or so.'

'Do we really hate one another that much?' Sue Smart asked.

'Yes,' Wade Frazer said.

Ignatz Thugg and Dr Babble helped elderly Mrs Rockingham to her feet. 'Oh dear,' she gasped, her withered and ancient face red, 'that was just simply dreadful! What a terrible, terrible place; I hope we never go there again.' Coming over, she plucked at Captain Belsnor's sleeve. 'We won't have to live through that again, will we? I do think, in all honesty, that life aboard the ship is far preferable to that wicked, uncivilized little place.'

'We won't be going back to Delmak-O,' Belsnor said.

'Thank heavens.' Mrs Rockingham seated herself; again Thugg and Dr Babble assisted her. 'Thank you,' she said to them. 'How kind of you. Could I have some coffee, Mr Morley?'

' "Coffee"?' he echoed and then he remembered; he was the ship's cook. All the precious food supplies, including coffee, tea and milk, were in his possession. 'I'll start a pot going,' he told them all.

In the kitchen he spooned heaping tablespoonfuls of good black ground coffee into the top of the pot. He noticed, then, as he had noticed many times before, that their store of coffee had begun to run low. In another few months they would be out entirely.

But this is a time at which coffee is needed, he decided, and continued to spoon the coffee into the pot. We are all shaken up, he realized. As never before.

His wife Mary entered the galley. 'What was the Building?'

'The Building.' He filled the coffee pot with reprocessed water. 'That was the Boeing plant on Proxima 10. Where the ship was built. Where we boarded it, remember? We were sixteen months at Boeing, getting trained, testing the ship, getting everything aboard and straightened out. Getting Persus 9 spaceworthy.'

Mary shivered and said, 'Those men in black leather uniforms.'

'I don't know,' Seth Morley said.

Ned Russell, the ship's MP, entered the galley. 'I can tell you what they were. The black leather guards were indications of our attempt to break it up and start again – they were directed by the thoughts of those who had "died".'

'You would know,' Mary said shortly.

'Easy,' Seth Morley said, putting his arm around her shoulder. From the start, many of them had not gotten along well with Russell. Which, considering his job, could have been anticipated.

'Someday, Russell,' Mary said, 'you're going to try to take over the ship . . . take it away from Captain Belsnor.'

'No,' Russell said mildly. 'All I'm interested in is keeping the peace. That's why I was sent here; that's what I intend to do. Whether anyone else wants me to or not.'

'I wish to God,' Seth Morley said, 'that there was really an Intercessor.' He still had trouble believing that they had made up Specktowsky's theology. 'At Tekel Upharsin,' he said, 'when the Walker-on-Earth came to me, it was so real. Even now it seems real. I can't shake it off.'

'That's why we created it,' Russell pointed out. 'Because we wanted it; because we didn't have it and needed to have it. Now we're back to reality, Morley; once again we have to face things as they are. It doesn't feel too good, does it?'

'No,' Seth Morley said.

Russell said, 'Do you wish you were back on Delmak-O?'

After a pause he said, 'Yes.'

'So do I,' Mary said, at last.

'I'm afraid,' Russell said, 'that I have to agree with you.

As bad as it was, as bad as we acted . . . at least there was hope. And back here on the ship—' He made a convulsive, savage, slashing motion. 'No hope. Nothing! Until we grow old like Roberta Rockingham and die.'

'Mrs Rockingham is lucky,' Mary said bitterly.

'Very lucky,' Russell said, and his face became swollen with impotence and bleak anger. And suffering.

SIXTEEN

After dinner that 'night' they gathered in the ship's control cabin. The time had come to plot out another polyencephalic world. To make it function it had to be a joint projection from all of them; otherwise, as in the final stages of the Delmak-O world, it would rapidly disintegrate.

In fifteen years they had become very skilled.

Especially Tony Dunkelwelt. Of his eighteen years, almost all had been spent aboard Persus 9. For him, the possession of polyencephalic worlds had become a normal way of life.

Captain Belsnor said, 'We didn't do so bad, in a way; we got rid of almost two weeks.'

'What about an aquatic world this time?' Maggie Walsh said. 'We could be dolphin-like mammals living in warm seas.'

'We did that,' Russell said. 'About eight months ago. Don't you remember it? Let's see . . . yes; we called it Aquasoma 3 and we stayed there three months of real time. A very successful world, I would say, and one of the most durable. Of course, back then we were less hostile.'

Seth Morley said, 'Excuse me.' He rose and walked from the ship's cabin into the narrow passageway.

There he stood, alone, rubbing his shoulder. A purely psychosomatic pain remained in it, a memory of Delmak-O which he would probably carry for a week. And that's all, he thought, that we have left of that particular world. Just a pain, plus a rapidly-fading memory.

How about a world, he thought, in which we lie good and dead, buried in our coffins? *That's what we really want.*

There had been no suicides aboard the ship for the last four years. Their population had become stabilized, at least temporarily.

Until Mrs Rockingham dies, he said to himself.

I wish I could go with her, he thought. How long, really, can we keep on? Not much longer. Thugg's wits are scrambled; so are Frazer's and Babble's. And me, too, he thought. Maybe I'm gradually breaking down, too. Wade Frazer is right; the murders on Delmak-O show how much derangement and hostility exists in all of us.

In that case, he thought suddenly, each escape world will be more feral . . . Russell is right. *It is a pattern.*

He thought, We will miss Roberta Rockingham when she dies; of us, she is the most benign and stable.

Because, he realized, she knows she is soon going to die.

Our only comfort. Death.

I could open vents here and there, he realized, and our atmosphere would be gone. Sucked out into the void. And then, more or less painlessly, we could all die. In one single, brief instant.

He placed his hand on the emergency release-lock of a nearby hatch vent. All I have to do, he said to himself, is move this thing counterclockwise.

He stood there, holding on to the release-lock, but doing nothing. What he intended to do had made him frozen, as if time had stopped. And everything around him looked two-dimensional.

A figure, coming down the corridor from the rear of the

ship, approached him. Bearded, with flowing, pale robes. A man, youthful and erect, with a pure, shining face.

'Walker,' Seth Morley said.

'No,' the figure said. 'I am not the Walker-on-Earth. I am the Intercessor.'

'But we invented you! We and TENCH 889B.'

The Intercessor said, 'I am here to take you away. Where would you like to go, Seth Morley? What would you like to be?'

'An illusion, you mean?' he said. 'Like our polyencephalic worlds?'

'No,' the Intercessor said. 'You will be free; you will die and be reborn. I will guide you to what you want, and to what is fitting and proper for you. Tell me what it is.'

'You don't want me to kill the others,' Seth Morley said, with abrupt comprehension. 'By opening the vents.'

The Intercessor inclined his head in a nod. 'It is for each of them to decide. You may decide only for yourself.'

'I'd like to be a desert plant,' Seth Morley said. 'That could see the sun all day. I want to be growing. Perhaps a cactus on some warm world. Where no one will bother me.'

'Agreed.'

'And sleep,' Seth Morley said. 'I want to be asleep but still aware of the sun and of myself.'

'That is the way with plants,' the Intercessor said. 'They sleep. And yet they know themselves to exist. Very well.' He held out his hand to Seth Morley. 'Come along.'

Reaching, Seth Morley touched the Intercessor's extended hand. Strong fingers closed around his own hand. He felt happy. He had never before been so glad.

'You will live and sleep for a thousand years,' the Intercessor said, and guided him away from where he stood, into the stars.

Mary Morley, stricken, said to Captain Belsnor, 'Captain, I can't find my husband.' She felt wet slow tears make their way down her cheeks. 'He's gone,' she said, in a half-wail.

'You mean he isn't on the ship anywhere?' Belsnor said. 'How could he get out without opening one of the hatches? They're the only way out of here, and if he opened one of the hatches our internal atmosphere would cease; we'd all be dead.'

'I know that,' she said.

'Then he still must be on the ship. We can search for him after we have our next polyencephalic world plotted out.'

'Now,' she said fiercely. 'Look for him *now*.'

'I can't,' Belsnor said.

Turning, she started away from him.

'Come back. You have to help.'

'I'm not coming back,' she said. She continued on, down the narrow corridor, into the galley. I think he was here last, she said to herself. I still sense him here, in the galley, where he spends so much of his time.

Huddled in the cramped little galley she heard their voices dim, gradually and slowly, into silence. They've gone into polyencephalic fusion again, she realized. Without me, this time. I hope they're happy now. This is the first time I haven't gone with them, she thought. I've missed out. What should I do? she asked herself. Where should I go?

Alone, she realized. Seth's gone; they're gone. And I can't make it by myself.

By degrees she crept back into the control cabin of the ship.

There they lay, in their individual cubicles, the many-wired cylinders covering their heads. All cylinders were in use except for hers . . . and for Seth's. She stood there, trembling with hesitation. What did they feed into the computer this time? she wondered. What are the premises, and what has TENCH 889B deduced from that?

What is the next world going to be like?

She examined the faintly-humming computer . . . but, of

all of them, only Glen Belsnor really knew how to operate it. They had of course used it, but she could not decipher the settings. The coded output baffled her, too; she remained by the computer, holding the punched tape in her hands . . . and then, with effort, made up her mind. It *must* be a reasonably good place, she told herself. We've built up so much skill, so much experience; it's not like the nightmare worlds we found ourselves in at first.

True, the homicidal element, the hostility, had grown. But the killings were not real. They were as illusory as killings in a dream.

And how easily they had taken place. How easy it had been for her to kill Susie Smart.

She lay down on the cot which belonged to her, anchored within her own particular cubicle, plugged in the life-protek mechanisms, and then, with relief, placed the cylinder over her head and shoulders. Its modulated hummm sounded faintly in her ears; a reassuring noise and one which she had heard so many times in the past, over the long and weary years.

Darkness covered her; she breathed it into herself, accepting it, demanding it . . . the darkness took over and, presently, she realized that it was night. She yearned, then, for daylight. For the world to be exposed – the new world which she could not yet see.

Who am I? she asked herself. Already it had become unclear in her mind. The *Persus 9*, the loss of Seth, their empty, trapped lives – all these faded from her like a burden released. She thought only of the daylight ahead; lifting her wrist to her face she tried to reach her watch. But it was not running. And she could not see.

She could make out stars, now, patterns of light interladen with drifts of nocturnal fog.

'Mrs Morley,' a fussy male voice said.

She opened her eyes, fully awake. Fred Gossim, Tekel Upharsin Kibbutz's top engineer, walked towards her carrying official papers. 'You got your transfer,' he told her;

he held out the papers and Mary Morley accepted them. 'You're going to a colony settlement on a planet called—' He hesitated, frowning. 'Delmar.'

'Delmak-O,' Mary Morley said, scanning the transfer orders. 'Yes – and I'm to go there by noser.' She wondered what kind of place Delmak-O was; she had never heard of it. And yet it sounded highly interesting; her curiosity had been stirred up. 'Did Seth get a transfer, too?' she asked.

' "Seth"?' Gossim raised an eyebrow. 'Who's "Seth"?'

She laughed. 'That's a very good question. I don't know. I guess it doesn't matter. I'm so glad to get this transfer—'

'Don't tell me about it,' Gossim said in his usual harsh way. 'As far as I am concerned you're abandoning your responsibilities to the kibbutz.' Turning, he stalked off.

A new life, Mary Morley said to herself. Opportunity and adventure and excitement. Will I like Delmak-O? she wondered. Yes. I know I will.

On light feet she danced towards her living area in the kibbutz's central building-complex. To begin to pack.